Go ahead and scream.

No one can hear you. You're no longer in the safe world you know.

You've taken a terrifying step . . .

into the darkest corners of your imagination.

You've opened the door to . . .

the NIGHTMARE rooM

The Howler

First published in the USA by Avon 2001
First published in Great Britain by Collins 2001
Collins is an imprint of HarperCollins*Publishers* Ltd,
77-85 Fulham Palace Road, Hammersmith, London, W6 8JB

The HarperCollins website address is www.fireandwater.com

1 3 5 7 9 8 6 4 2

ISBN 0 00 710455 3

Printed and bound in Great Britain by
Omnia Books Limited, Glasgow

the NiGHTMARE room

The Howler

R.L. STINE

PARACHUTE PRESS

An imprint of HarperCollinsPublishers

Welcome...

I'm R.L. Stine. This month I have a story for you about a boy who *wishes* his house was haunted!

That's him huddled in his room, turning the dials of a strange, little machine called *The Howler*. His name is Spencer Turner, and he just bought the gadget at a ghost supply store. Will it pick up the howls of real ghosts?

Spencer is desperate to talk to a ghost. There's just one problem. Sometimes it's best not to disturb a howling ghost. He may be howling because he's *real angry*!

Be careful, Spencer. You may not find the ghost you seek. But you may find *yourself* haunting *THE NIGHTMARE ROOM*.

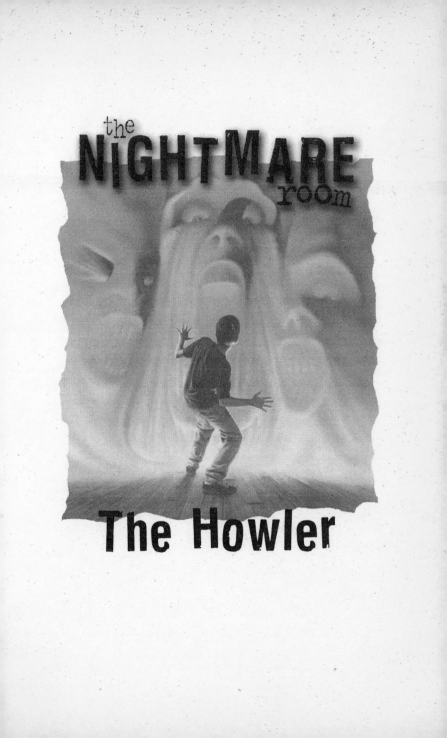

the NIGHTMARE room

The Howler

Do you believe in ghosts?

I didn't believe in them for most of my life. But ever since last winter, I want to believe.

It's my dream, my most important wish. I think about it every day.

I want to see a ghost. I want to talk to a ghost.

The ghost's name is Ian.

I remember every detail of that frosty cold day last December. The snow was deep, and it had a crust on top that crunched when we walked on it.

The sun hung low over the trees. It made the snow gleam like a sheet of silver. Snow clung to the branches of the evergreen trees, and the hedges were topped with blankets of white.

I remember the frozen air burning my cheeks. The fat, puffy clouds floating like snowmen high in the bright sky.

We carried our skates to Wellman Lake, a block

1

from my house. It's not really a lake. It's only a pond.

My friend Vanessa was there. We teased her about her pink snowsuit. Such a babyish color. She didn't care. She said it was made with real goose down and kept her very warm.

I remember Vanessa's red hair glowing in the sunlight. And the reflection of the snow in her green eyes.

Scott came along too. Chubby, red-faced Scott, with his black hair wild about his head like a furry hat.

He lives in the run-down old house next door to mine. He was bragging about his new CD player, and kicking snow on us, and telling dumb jokes.

Typical Scott.

I didn't invite Scott to join us. I don't like him very much. Neither does Vanessa.

He's so loud, and always bragging. And he always wants to pick fights and make bets about stupid things no one else cares about.

I think Scott has a special radar. Or else he spies on my house all day. Because whenever I go out, there he is. He comes running from his house, ready to join in.

So there were four of us that day. My cousin Ian was the fourth. His family was staying with us for a few days before going on to Florida for Christmas.

I was happy to see him. Ian was my age, thirteen. And even though we didn't see each other very often, we always got along really well. We were like brothers.

Yes, I already have a brother. Big Jerk Nick.

Nick is three years older than me. And he treats me like an insect he wants to squash under his shoe.

Nick says that in every family, the big brother is the boss and the little brother is the slave. It sounds stupid, but Nick really believes it.

So, it's "Spencer, go to the kitchen and make me a sandwich." And "Spencer, I have to go out. Type this homework into the computer for me."

"Spencer, bring me a Coke. Spencer, go see who's at the door. Spencer, get a move on!"

Nick is a lot bigger than me. And he works out. And he's on the wrestling team at school. So I try very hard to stay out of his way.

And that's one reason I liked to think of Ian as a brother.

And now, just about every day, I remember Ian walking with us to the lake. His boots crunched on the crusty snow. And the ice skates I found for him bounced on the shoulders of his down vest as we trudged up the hill on Marlowe Street.

Ian looked a lot like me. Dark brown hair. Brown eyes. Serious face. Average height. Kind of skinny.

He had a lot of energy. He was always bouncing up and down and drumming his fingers on things. He couldn't stand or sit still for a minute.

I remember we were passing the low stone wall in front of the Faulkners' house. The top of the wall was iced up. Vanessa, Scott, and I started to walk beside it.

But Ian leaped onto the top of the wall. He did a crazy balancing act, slipping and sliding. His arms waved wildly above his head.

We screamed at him to jump down. But he only laughed. He was still laughing when he fell off. Luckily, he fell onto his back in a soft clump of snow-covered bushes.

Luckily.

Thinking about it now makes me feel really sad.

I guess that was the only lucky thing that happened that day.

I remember the gray-white ice that covered the lake—so smooth and glassy. Several cawing black birds took off from the ice when they saw us coming.

A clump of snow fell off an evergreen branch and shattered over the ice. I remember the soft *thud* it made.

So many sounds I remember from that day. Some of them so horrifying, I want to hold my ears and shut them out forever.

We hurried to pull on our skates. Scott insisted on making us all take off our gloves and run our fingers over the blades on his new skates. He said they were made of titanium, which made them stronger and faster than any other ice skates.

Ian had trouble with a knot in his laces. The skates weren't his. They were a pair that Nick couldn't wear anymore. So they didn't fit Ian that well.

Vanessa helped him with the knot. Then she was the first one onto the ice.

Vanessa is a very graceful skater. She skates like a pro. She's a natural athlete. She's a forward on the girls' basketball team at school. And she does track.

But she says she's not really into sports. She would rather stay in the studio her parents made for her in their garage and paint. She wants to be an artist someday.

I watched Ian go slipping and sliding onto the lake. His legs were wobbling like crazy, and he went down laughing, skidding on his stomach. "These skates won't work, Spencer," he called to me. "I can't lace them tight enough."

"Have you ever ice-skated before?" I called.

He laughed again. "Not really!"

He pulled down his wool ski cap. And then he was on his feet and skating unsteadily toward Vanessa. She grabbed his hand and guided him slowly over the ice.

Soon, all four of us were skating. I leaned into the wind, my face burning from the cold. I pressed my gloved hands on my knees and moved beside Vanessa and Ian.

We were all gliding easily now. It felt so great. The frozen lake shimmered beneath us. The cold air smelled fresh and sweet. The fat white clouds were so pretty against the sky.

"We need music," Scott declared. He was skating backward, doing fast loops, showing off as usual.

None of us had brought a radio. So we started to

sing. We sang some songs we knew from the radio and skated along to them. We were singing and laughing at the same time.

When did it all go wrong?

I guess it started when Scott swiped Ian's wool cap off his head. "Keep away!" he shouted, tossing the cap to me.

I missed it and it slid across the ice. Ian and I both swooped toward it. But I came up with it and heaved it to Vanessa.

"Hey—give it back!" Ian shouted. His face was bright red from the cold. His dark hair was wet and matted to his forehead.

He made a wild grab for the cap. Laughing, Vanessa held it up in front of him, then tossed it to Scott.

Scott leaped for it. Started to fall. The cap flew onto the ice right in front of Ian.

He grabbed it up and skated away from us. "You guys aren't funny," he said. He leaned forward and skated away.

He still had the black cap in his hands when the ice started to crack.

It made a loud, long, ripping sound. Another sound I'll never forget.

I saw the ice breaking under Ian's skates. I didn't even have time to shout.

I saw a long block of ice slant up. I saw Ian's shocked expression. Saw his hands fly up.

Water splashed onto the ice. Another loud *craaaack* echoed off the trees.

Ian started to drop.

It happened so fast, so terrifyingly fast.

I saw his legs sink into the hole in the ice. More water splashed up. His head disappeared. His hands groped for the surface.

His black cap sat on the cracked ice like a small, dark animal.

But Ian was gone.

"NOOOOOOOOOO!" Was that *me* screaming like that?

I don't remember screaming. And I don't remember skating.

But before I realized it, I was racing to the broken ice, racing to the hole, racing to rescue my cousin.

And then I was on my knees. Leaning over the hole, peering into the dark, splashing water. Shouting his name over and over. "Ian! Ian! Ian!"

I cried out when his hand appeared. Like a pale fish in the dark, tossing water.

I grabbed his hand. Already so cold.

"Ian! Ian! Ian!"

I was on my stomach, leaning over the jagged hole. On my stomach, holding on to Ian's hand. Tugging. Pulling with all my strength.

The hand so cold. So slippery.

"Ian! Ian! Ian!"

I had him. I had his hand. I gave it a hard jerk.

"Ian—your head! Where is your head? Lift your head out! Ian—please!"

His hand started to slip from mine.

I grabbed his wrist, grabbed it with both hands.

"Ian—I—I can't hold on! I—"

Another *crack*.

I felt the ice move beneath me.

A fat plank of ice rose up in front of me. And then the ice below me dropped.

I let out a terrified cry.

I struggled to hold on. Struggled with all my strength.

But Ian's hand fell away. Fell so lightly, it didn't make a splash.

And then I dropped. Headfirst. Headfirst into the dark, frozen, churning water.

The last thing I saw was the black cap, still sitting safely on the ice. Ian's black cap, safe and sound.

And then I plunged down.

Down . . . down into darkness.

I don't remember the rest. It's all a cold blue blur.

I don't remember being pulled from the water. I don't remember the crowd of people from the houses that face the lake. The police. The firefighters. My crying friends. My terrified family running across the snow without coats or hats.

When I was safe and sound at home, they told me the story of my rescue. But I didn't remember any of it.

I remembered Ian's hand slipping away so silently.

And then the cold, hard slap of the water. And the heavy, thick darkness rising around me. Pulling me deeper . . . deeper.

That's all. That's all I remember.

I came home and Ian didn't.

And ever since that day last winter, I haven't gone back to the lake. I *can't* go back to the lake.

My friends still go swimming there in the summer. And now that winter has come again, the frozen surface is filled with ice-skaters.

I can see the lake from my bedroom. Some nights I gaze out at it, all shimmery under the moonlight.

And I feel so sad . . . so sad. I have to turn away and pull my window shade down.

I'll never go back there. Never.

Ever since that day, I've wanted to believe in ghosts.

With all my heart, I wanted ghosts to be real. I wanted to contact a ghost. I wanted to talk to a ghost.

I want to find Ian's ghost. I'm *desperate* to find my cousin's ghost.

Because I want him to know how I still think about him every day. And I want him to know how hard I tried to save him.

Does he know that I tried? Does he know that I risked my life for him?

Does he forgive me for not pulling him out?

I've spent the last year trying to find him.

I haven't told my parents. I don't want them to start worrying about me.

When they are around, I pretend everything is fine. But I desperately want to find my cousin.

And now I've found a little machine that might do the job. It's called a specter detector, and I ordered it online.

It's a square gray box with one button and some lights on it. It looks a lot like a phone modem.

It took me a long time to hook the thing up to my computer. The connecting cable didn't quite fit. But I finally managed it. And the green light on the box started blinking away.

I sat down at the keyboard and started to type in the codes from the instruction book.

"This isn't going to work, Spencer," Vanessa said. She sighed, leaning over my shoulder. "You've got to stop buying these crazy contraptions."

I kept typing, my eyes on the monitor screen. "But it comes from the Ghost Warehouse," I said. "This is supposed to be the same machine that was used in *Ghostbusters*."

"But that was a *movie*!" Vanessa protested. "It wasn't real. It was all special effects."

"I know," I said. "But what if—"

Vanessa spun my desk chair around so that I was facing her. "Spencer, you've got to stop this," she said. "How much money have you spent on these crazy ghost-finding machines? You buy these things, and you get your hopes up. And then each time you're so disappointed."

"I know, I know," I groaned. "But what if this one works?"

I spun back around to the computer. The green and red lights on the specter detector were blinking like crazy now. The monitor screen glowed yellow, then black. Yellow, then black.

Come on—work! I silently prayed. *Please work!*

The lights blinked furiously.

Vanessa sighed again. "This is crazy, Spencer. You're wasting your time, and you know it."

"Watch the screen," I said, pointing. "Look. Something is taking shape there." I leaned as close as I could.

"Spencer! Hey—punk!"

Nick's shout made me jump. Punk. That's what he calls me when he's being nice.

"Hey—punk!" he called from his room down the hall. "Run downstairs and make me a bowl of corn flakes."

"I'm . . . kind of busy!" I called back.

"Not too much milk!" Nick shouted. "I like it dry. With lots of sugar."

"Why can't he get his own cereal?" Vanessa whispered, making a disgusted face.

"Because he doesn't have to. He has me," I whispered back.

13

"Hurry, punk!" Nick shouted.

I watched the shadows shifting on the glowing monitor. "Give me a few minutes!" I yelled.

"Hey—" Nick called. "Which way do you like your nose to point—down or up? Because I'm going to fix it for you right now!"

"Okay, okay!" I jumped to my feet. I knew Nick wasn't kidding. He would love to move my face around and leave an ear where my nose should be.

"Watch the screen," I told Vanessa. I ran downstairs to the kitchen and made my brother a bowl of corn flakes. I heaped three teaspoons of sugar on it. And poured in just a splash of milk.

Then I ran breathlessly back upstairs and into his room. Nick was sprawled on his bed, reading a sports magazine. He took the bowl from me with a grunt. No word of thank you. He *never* says thank you.

"Get out of my room," he muttered. "How many times do I have to tell you to stay out of my room?"

"You're welcome," I said sarcastically.

I hurried back to my room and slammed the door. "Anything happening?" I asked Vanessa. I brushed her out of my desk chair.

"It's all a fake, Spencer," she said. "It just makes eerie colors on the screen, and the lights blink. It doesn't do anything else. It doesn't detect ghosts."

"Well . . . let me try something else," I said. I opened the instruction book and found another set of codes. As I typed them in, the little gray box started to hum. The lights began to blink furiously.

"Give it up," Vanessa groaned. "It's another fake. Just another fake."

"No. Wait," I insisted. "It says on the box it's guaranteed. Just wait. Give it a chance. Something is happening."

The box hummed louder.

A yellow light began to blink.

The monitor screen began to blink too.

Behind me, I heard a *click*.

A *creak*.

I turned to Vanessa—and something behind her caught my eye. "Look—" I whispered.

She turned and we both stared at my bedroom door.

Slowly, slowly, the door was sliding open.

"I knew it would work," I whispered. "I knew it."

I held my breath and watched as the door slowly, silently, swung open.

"Wh-who's there?" I choked out.

"It's me," a voice said.

And Scott stepped into the room. He stopped when he saw our shocked faces. "Hey—what's your problem?" he asked.

Vanessa burst out laughing. "Spencer thought you were a ghost," she said.

Scott rolled his eyes. "Yeah. Sure." He stepped up to the computer and picked up the specter detector. "What's this? A new game player? What kind of games do you have for it?"

"It's not a game," I snapped, grabbing it away from him.

"It's another ghost detector," Vanessa said. "But it doesn't work."

Scott dropped onto my bed. He picked up my pillow and squeezed it between his hands. Then he bounced up and down as he stared at the monitor.

"Why do you keep wasting your time, Spencer? I

keep telling you, my house is haunted. There are ghosts all over the place."

"Scott—please don't start that again," I begged.

"Yeah, Scott," Vanessa agreed. "Please don't start that."

"But it's *true!*" he protested.

After I became interested in ghosts, Scott started bragging that his house was haunted. He was always coming into school and telling everyone how a ghost kept him up all night. Or how he spotted a ghost in the basement or the attic.

A few kids believed him. But I knew he was lying.

I knew what he was doing. He just wanted attention. He always had to be the first one to do this, and the first one to do that.

And now he wanted to make sure he was the first one to see a ghost.

It was kind of sad, really. Why did he have to be the center of attention? Why did he feel he had to lie and brag and make up stories so that kids would like him?

"Come over here," he said, jumping up from my bed. He tossed my pillow against the wall. Then he pulled me up from my chair and dragged me to my bedroom window.

"Check out my house," he said, grabbing the sides of my head and turning it to face his house. "Look at the broken shutters. The faded shingles. The sagging roof. The dark attic windows. It *looks* like a haunted house, doesn't it?"

"It just looks old," I said. I jerked my head, trying to knock his hands away. "Just because it's old and a little run-down doesn't mean it's a haunted house, Scott."

He groaned. He wouldn't let go of my head. "Look at it," he insisted. "No lie. I've seen ghosts in there. I hear them at night, clanking up and down in the attic."

"Give me a break," I sighed.

"Give us both a break," Vanessa chimed in.

Scott had no idea how serious this was to me. I really couldn't stand to hear any more of his phony ghost stories. I decided to end his ghost talk forever.

"Okay," I said. "Show us. Show us your ghosts—right now."

Scott's cheeks turned pink. "Uh . . . I can't right now," he said, staring down at the floor.

"Why not?" I demanded.

"My mom has her book club over," he replied. "And I'm not supposed to bother her." He shoved his hands into his jeans pockets. "How about tomorrow?"

I turned to Vanessa. "Is tomorrow okay?"

She nodded. "I guess. But it's a total waste of time. You know he doesn't have any ghosts at his house. He's making it all up."

"No way," Scott insisted. "I'll prove it to you. After school tomorrow." He hurried away.

The gray box buzzed. I spun away from the window and hurried back to the computer. The screen had gone black. The red and green lights had stopped blinking.

"I can't believe you bought this stupid thing,"

Vanessa said. "It's just a toy. That's all."

I shrugged. "Whatever."

I thought about Scott's ghosts all through school the next day. I knew there was no way he could show us any ghosts. I wondered what excuse he would give.

Vanessa and I reached his house a little after three-thirty. He pushed open the back door, and we stepped into the kitchen. I inhaled deeply. "Wow, it smells good in here."

"My mom is roasting a chicken," Scott said.

"Do the ghosts like your mom's cooking?" Vanessa asked.

It was a joke. But Scott answered seriously, "I've never seen them eat. Sometimes they move the plates around, and we find them in different cabinets. But we've never had any food missing."

I squinted at Scott. Was he for real?

No way, I decided. Scott will do anything to be the center of attention.

And then I heard the howl. High and shrill.

A ghostly howl. So near . . . So near . . .

I gasped and turned to Vanessa. She'd heard it too.

My eyes darted around the room. And I heard it again.

A raspy howl, followed by eerie scratching sounds.

The howl of a ghost.

Another eerie howl floated into the room. Then more scratching sounds.

"Scott—let the cat in!" Scott's mom called from the other room. "She's at the back door again. Don't you hear her?"

"I'll get her, Mom," Scott called. He trotted to the door. "Dumb cat," he muttered.

I let out a long sigh.

Vanessa laughed. "Did you think you heard a ghost?"

"No. Of course not," I lied. "I knew it was a cat." I could feel my face growing hot. I always blush whenever I tell a lie.

I felt a little shaky. Why did I suddenly think Scott really had ghosts in his house?

I guess it was because I wanted to believe *so much*.

Matilda, Scott's black cat, came running over our feet, desperate to get to her water dish. Scott appeared in the kitchen doorway. "Come on. We don't want to keep the ghosts waiting."

We followed him through the front hall to the stairs. The hall was long and dark, with ghostly gray wallpaper and lights on the walls shaped like candles.

"Scott—who is here?" his mother shouted from the living room.

"It's Spencer and Vanessa," he called to her. And then he added in a deep voice that was supposed to be scary, "They've come to visit the Haunted Mansion."

"Huh?" his mother called. "Haunted *what*?"

"She tries to keep the ghosts a secret," Scott whispered to us. "She doesn't want anyone to know about them."

"Yeah. Sure," I muttered.

The wooden stairs creaked and groaned as Vanessa and I followed him upstairs. "Sometimes I hear footsteps going up and down these stairs late at night," Scott said. "I flash on the lights—and there's no one here."

Vanessa shook her head. "He's good," she whispered. "He's real good. He almost has *me* believing!"

"Not me," I whispered back.

In the upstairs hall, we stopped under a door in the ceiling. Scott grabbed a rope that hung down from the door.

"This leads to the attic," he said. "I think this is where the ghosts hang out before dark."

He tugged the rope. The door creaked down. There were wooden stairs built on the other side of the door. "Careful. Some of these stairs are rotted," Scott warned.

I started up the stairs slowly, one at a time. The stairs were steep, and there was no bannister to hold on to.

Halfway up, I turned back to Scott. "You're telling us we'll see ghosts here?"

He nodded solemnly. "They're not shy. They're not afraid of us. They don't care if we see them or not."

I climbed the rest of the way and waited for Vanessa and Scott to join me. The attic was long and low-ceilinged. It was one big L-shaped room that curved off to the right.

There was one window, smeared with a thick layer of dust. Orange sunlight seeped through, but it lit only a small part of the room. The rest of the attic lay in shadow.

I blinked several times, waiting for my eyes to adjust to the strange light. The attic was cluttered with cartons and stacks of magazines, books, and furniture. I saw couches and chairs covered in sheets, like Halloween ghosts.

Cobwebs clung to an old coatrack, tilted against one wall. A stack of framed photographs leaned against the opposite wall. The photos were dark, the paper yellowed and cracked.

In one of the photos, a strange-looking boy in a black cap appeared to stare out at us. He had dark circles around his sad eyes. His face was puckered like a prune. He looked more like a monkey than a boy.

"Is that your baby picture?" Vanessa joked to Scott.

He raised a finger to his lips. "Shhhh. Do you want to see a ghost or not?"

We stepped out of the light into the shadowy area of the room. My shoes slid on the thick layer of dust over the floor. I tripped over a small table but caught it before it fell.

We turned the corner. I squinted to see. This section of the attic was totally dark.

Scott pulled a light cord. A tiny ceiling bulb flickered on.

In the dim light, I saw an old rocking chair with one arm broken. A wooden clock lying on its side. A stack of dishes.

And then . . .

And then . . .

Vanessa and I saw her at the same time. An old woman—so pale, her face so ghostly pale—standing against the curtained back wall. Her old-fashioned clothes were faded. No color. No color anywhere.

My mouth dropped open. A tiny cry burst out.

Vanessa grabbed my hand. "Scott wasn't kidding!" she whispered.

I swallowed. Was I really seeing a ghost?

The old woman stared out at us with glassy eyes. She seemed to stare into the distance, as if watching for someone else.

She stood so still. Her faded blouse was tattered and stained. A faded brown hat covered her hair. Her hands were hidden in the ragged pleats of the long, old-fashioned skirt.

"I—I don't believe it," I murmured. I realized I was trembling.

Scott reached for the light switch. "Let's leave her in peace," he whispered.

"No, wait," Vanessa said. She took a few steps forward.

"No—stop!" Scott grabbed her. "Don't go any closer. She might be dangerous."

Vanessa pulled away from him. She stepped closer to the ghost.

"Stop!" Scott cried.

Too late. Vanessa stepped up to the ghost—and pulled off her head.

"Huh?" I gasped. "It's . . . it's a dummy?"

Vanessa laughed. "It took you long enough, Spencer!" she declared. "I knew it was a dummy as soon as I saw it."

Scott laughed. "I gotcha good, Spencer. You should have seen the look on your face!"

He took the wooden head from Vanessa and placed it back on top of the body. "Actually, it's an old dress dummy my parents found up here when we moved in. Women used it for sewing dresses and stuff. Dad put the head on it a couple of Halloweens ago."

He pointed at me and laughed loudly again. "Suck-er!"

I let out a sigh. I felt like a total jerk. What could be worse than being fooled by that idiot Scott?

The whole school would hear about it by tomorrow, I knew.

I angrily kicked a carton out of my way and started toward the steps. I stormed out of his house and ran across the driveway to my yard. My hands were balled into angry fists. I wanted to go back and punch Scott's fat face until *he* was a ghost.

I *hated* feeling like such a jerk. But I knew it was because I needed to believe. I was so desperate to contact Ian, I'd even believe Scott!

Vanessa came running after me. She stopped me

halfway through my kitchen door. "Lighten up, Spencer," she said. "You've just got to get over this ghost thing. Just forget about it."

When I turned to her, I suddenly felt like crying. "I . . . I don't think I can," I whispered.

That night, I think I saw Ian's ghost.

After dinner, I was fiddling with the specter detector, when Nick burst into my room. He shoved the end of a candy bar into his mouth and tossed the wrapper onto my floor.

"What's that?" he asked, chewing noisily. Chocolate ran down over his chin.

"It's nothing," I muttered. I wasn't in the mood to fight with him.

"It's another ghost detector—isn't it!" Nick said. He grinned at me. He had chocolate stuck to his teeth. "You know what you are, Spencer? You are one of those loonies. You've become a nutcase."

"Takes one to know one," I muttered.

"You're out there. You're really out there," Nick said, still grinning. "You're out there searching for ghosts and goblins, right? With all the other nutcases. Ooh—look out, Spencer. You'd better search for UFOs too. You might find a UFO, Spencer. Wouldn't that be a thrill?"

"Give me a break," I groaned. I really don't—"

"Look out!" he shouted. "I see something. Oh, no! *Duck!* Here comes a UFF!"

And he slapped me in the back of the head—so hard, I went sailing off my chair.

"Hey—stop it!" I shouted.

"Didn't you see it coming? You got hit by a UFF! Unidentified Flying Fist." He laughed as if he'd just made the funniest joke in the world.

I rubbed the back of my head. "You're a total creep," I muttered.

"Don't sit there. You could be in the path of another UFF," Nick warned. "Go downstairs and make me a sandwich."

"Huh? A sandwich? We just ate dinner an hour ago!" I said.

"Yeah. A whole hour ago," he repeated. He raised his hand. "Better hurry. Here comes another UFF."

I climbed unhappily to my feet. "What kind of sandwich?" I groaned.

"Don't ever ask me what kind," Nick snapped. "Just make sure it's something good."

He swung his hand, trying to slap me again as I passed by him. But I ducked, and the slap only brushed the top of my hair.

Out in the hall, I turned and yelled back to him. "I could use a little support, you know!"

He burped really loud in reply. Nice guy, huh?

But then, at least, he took the sandwich I made to

his room and didn't pester me for the rest of the night.

I spent another hour or so discovering what I already knew—the specter detector was a piece of junk. I unplugged it and heaved it into the trash.

A little before eleven, I changed into pajamas. The winter wind rattled the panes in my bedroom window. I stepped over to the window and peered out.

From my window, I could see the tops of the snow-covered evergreen trees around the shore of Wellman Lake. And I could see a wide section of the frozen lake. The ice glowed dully under the light of a bright half-moon.

On moonless nights it was too dark to see the lake. On those nights, it looked like an enormous black pit stretching beyond the trees.

A deep, dark pit.

That's what the lake was. A deep, dark pit that could hold a person forever.

I pressed my forehead against the cold glass and gazed out. My eyes swept over the snow-covered yards. The streets had been plowed earlier that afternoon. High banks of snow lined the curbs.

The wind shook the panes again. The dark trees outside seemed to shiver.

And then just beyond the trees, on the shimmering gray surface of the icy lake, something caught my eye. Something moving across the lake.

Something glowing, moving rapidly, steadily. The glow slid between the trees.

I raised my hands to the sides of my face and gazed harder.

And saw a boy gliding across the ice. Glistening, a soft blue light surrounding him. Such a cold light sweeping around him as he glided so smoothly over the frozen lake.

All by himself, a boy, glowing against the darkness. Skating so smoothly, so sweetly.

"Ian—is that you?" I said out loud. My heart pounding. My whole body trembling as I continued to stare out.

"Ian—it *is* you—isn't it! Don't move! Don't leave! I'm coming!"

I whirled away from the window and hurried to get dressed.

I was still tugging on my coat as I raced outside. A burst of frozen air greeted me.

It had been snowing for two days. My boots sank into the powdery snow. The wind blew snow down from the trees as I started to run.

I glanced back at the house. I saw a light in my parents' room. Did they hear me go out? Maybe I should have told them, I thought.

But they would ask why. And then I'd have to explain.

And then they would think I'm crazy.

They think my interest in ghosts is just a hobby. A stage I'm going through. Something I will grow out of.

They don't know the real reason I want to believe in ghosts. They don't know how desperate I am to find my cousin.

"Ian? Hey—Ian?" I cupped my hands around my mouth and shouted his name as I ran through the dark, snow-covered evergreen trees to the lakeshore.

Gusts of wind sent powdery snow blowing over the icy lake. The snow swirled up, forming weird shapes, like ghosts rising from the ice. Under the light of the half-moon, the trees cast long shadows stretching over the surface.

"Ian? Are you here?" My voice was muffled in the wind.

I searched the ice for the blue light. For the boy skating so smoothly inside the glow. But the silver-gray ice reflected only the dark, shifting shadows.

"Ian?"

I stopped. My throat tightened. I suddenly had trouble breathing.

I haven't been here in a year, I thought.

I haven't stood here since that horrible day.

A wave of fright swept over me. I felt paralyzed. I had the strange feeling that I could no longer move. That I would never move again.

But Ian was here. I *knew* he was. I had seen him.

Without even realizing it, I took a few steps onto the ice.

Only darkness now. And the howl of the wind. The creak of tree branches. Snow flying over the frozen lake.

I took a few more steps. The ice was hard and solid under my boots.

"Ian? Are you here?" I called. "It's me—Spencer!"

The wind swept around me. A cold blast of air

blew down the collar of my coat, sending a chill along the back of my neck.

I shielded my eyes from the moonlight and squinted across the ice, searching for the blue glow. "Ian?"

I took a few more steps. And then my boot slid over something. A bump in the ice.

Before I could catch my balance, I had fallen to my knees. I gasped when I saw the slender tracks. Two lines cut into the fresh powder of snow.

Ice-skate tracks.

"Hey!" Bending low to see them clearly, I began to follow the tracks. They led me in a wide circle.

The tracks were fresh. Sharp and clean. They had to be made just minutes ago. The twin tracks curved in a broad circle. Then they turned and led straight out to the center of the lake.

Were these Ian's tracks? The tracks of his ghost?

The thought started my shivers again. I pulled my coat tighter and forced my trembling legs to keep moving.

"Oh, wow." I stopped and stared down, blinking at the ice. The tracks stopped.

They ended at a low drift of snow. Just ended.

I brushed the snow away with both hands. No skate marks on the ice beneath it. I stood up and walked in a wide circle, trying to find where the tracks began again.

But they didn't. They just ended. As if the skater

suddenly floated off the lake, up to the sky.

Or sank below the ice.

Shuddering, my teeth chattering, I turned away. The evergreen trees suddenly appeared far away. I didn't realize I had followed the tracks so far out onto the ice.

The gusting wind grew sharper, burning my cheeks. Snow blew around my boots, my legs.

I heard a creaking sound.

Was the ice too thin this far out? Was it starting to crack under my weight?

"No. Please," I whispered.

Carefully, I started to make my way back toward shore.

I heard another *creak*. So close behind me.

I leaned forward into the wind and began to skate, sliding my boots over the snowy ice, taking long strides.

The trees still seemed so far in the distance. The wind blew harder, as if trying to keep me from the shore.

Another *creak*. A cracking sound. So loud, so close.

I sucked in a deep breath and forced myself forward.

One sliding step . . . another . . . another.

"NOOOOOOOO!" I let out a shriek of horror as a hand reached up from the cracking ice—and grabbed me by the ankle.

"AAAGGGH!" A scream of horror burst from my throat.

I kicked hard. And fell.

My hands hit the ice first, sending pain jolting down my arms.

I landed on my stomach. Struggled to my knees. Spun around, gasping, panting like an animal.

I screamed again when I saw the hand gripped around my ankle.

No. Wait . . .

Not a hand. Not a hand reaching up from the frozen depths of the lake.

My whole body shook wildly as I plucked it off my leg. A glove. A dark leather glove. Probably left on the ice by a skater.

I brought the glove close to my face and studied it. It sagged, limp in my fingers.

But . . . it had *gripped* me! A moment before, it was hard and firm. I had felt it tighten around my ankle.

But how could that be?

With a shuddering cry, I tossed it away. Tossed it across the ice.

Then I scrambled home.

I climbed into bed and pulled the covers up to my chin. But I couldn't stop shaking.

I can't go back there, I told myself. I can't. It's too terrifying.

But I saw something. Those tracks in the ice. The blue glow. I saw something.

Ian—was it you?

I'll keep trying to find you. I promise.

After school the next day, I met Vanessa in front of her locker. We had planned to walk into town. Vanessa wanted to buy some art supplies for a new painting she was working on.

She hoisted her backpack onto her shoulders and zipped up her bright red parka. "How's it going?"

I rolled my eyes. "Don't ask. Scott told everyone in school about how I freaked when I saw the dummy in his attic. Everywhere I go, I see kids laughing at me."

Vanessa tsk-tsked. "Scott is such a jerk."

I turned and saw him trotting down the hall toward us. "Come on—hurry!" I cried. I pulled Vanessa to the front doors. We burst outside and started to run.

The sky was gray, filled with thick black clouds

threatening more snow. A sharp wind forced me back a step. I lowered my head and kept running.

"Wait up!" I heard Scott calling from the steps in front of the school. "I just saw a ghost!" His laughter floated after us.

I picked up speed, turned, and ducked into the narrow alley that led away from the playground.

"Where are you going?" Vanessa cried breathlessly. Her breath rose up in white puffs in front of her.

"I don't care," I said. "I have to get away from Scott!"

The alley was narrow. It ran along the backyards of houses on either side. Trash cans stood outside low fences. Stacks of old newspapers, covered in snow, were piled beside them.

"Stop running," Vanessa demanded, trotting beside me. "What are we doing in this alley? We never go this way. You can stop. Scott isn't following us."

"I want to keep running forever," I said. "Everyone was laughing at me today. Everyone."

"So what are you going to do?" Vanessa demanded. "Run away from home because Scott played a dumb trick on you, and now kids are teasing you about it?" She grabbed my coat sleeve and pulled me to a stop.

I kicked a clump of snow. "I don't know. I hate being the joke of the school. But—"

I blinked. Snow from a tree overhead had fallen

onto my forehead. I brushed it away—and stared at the little store across the street.

"Where are we?" I asked. We had come out on a block I didn't recognize.

"I think this is Oak. Or maybe it's Chambers," Vanessa said. "I never use that alley, so—"

The store caught her eye too. It looked more like a house than a store, with faded gray shingles and shutters painted black. I squinted at the sign above the door: LITTLE HOUSE OF SPIRITS.

"What is that store?" I asked. "Is it new?"

We crossed the street. I led the way onto the small front stoop. "Is it open?" Vanessa asked. "It doesn't look as if it's open."

I peered into the window. There was no display. No hint of what the store sold. And then I spotted a small hand-lettered sign: GHOST SUPPLIES.

"Huh?" I let out a gasp. "Is this for real?"

Vanessa tugged my arm. "Let's go, Spencer. You know it isn't for real."

I gazed at the little sign. GHOST SUPPLIES . . .

"You know that stuff is a waste of money," Vanessa insisted.

I grabbed the door handle. "Come on. Let's just see what they have," I said.

I pushed open the door. A bell attached to the other side rang as the door swung open. Kicking snow off my boots, I stepped into a dimly lit hallway.

Vanessa bumped up behind me. "It's dark in here," she whispered. "Do you think they're open?"

I took a few steps into the front room. A small desk, cluttered with papers, stood against one wall. Two long rows of dark display cases faced the desk.

"Anyone here?" I called.

"Let's go," Vanessa whispered. "This place is creeping me out. I don't think it's a real store."

I stared at the tall display cases. What did they hold? It was too dark to see.

"Okay. They must be closed," I said. I turned to go.

Then I heard someone cough. A back door opened, spilling yellow light into the room.

A man stepped out. He was very short. Very thin and weary-looking. Sort of stooped over, as if he didn't have the strength to stand up straight.

He had shiny white hair pulled behind his head in a long ponytail. As he came closer, I could see the square-shaped eyeglasses resting low on his long, slender nose.

Even in the dim light, I could see how pale he was. He smiled a thin smile, his gray eyes moving from Vanessa to me. He walked slowly, with a slight limp. He seemed so fragile.

"Come in," he said. I expected a tiny, frail voice. But his voice was booming and deep. "Welcome to the Little House of Spirits."

"Are—are you open?" I stammered.

His smile grew wider, making his pale cheeks crease up into thousands of tiny lines. "I'm always open. The spirits never rest. And neither do I."

He leaned back against the desk and tugged at his long white ponytail. "Are you looking for ghost traps?"

I stared at him. "Uh . . . what?"

"You want to get rid of ghosts? I have a very popular product called Ghost-Proof. It comes in a spray can."

"No," I replied. "My house isn't haunted."

He nodded. "Most people come here for traps or alarms. They have unwanted ghosts to chase away." He squinted at me over the square glasses. "Did your parents send you? Were they embarrassed to come here themselves?"

"No," I said. "My parents don't believe in ghosts."

He pulled himself up straight. "And you want to prove to them that ghosts really do exist?"

"No," I said. I glanced at Vanessa. She looked really uncomfortable. She signaled with her eyes toward the door.

I turned back to the strange little man. "I'm trying to find a ghost," I blurted out.

"Ah-ha!" he declared. He rubbed his thin hands together. "You want to find a ghost who lives in your house?"

"I don't even know if he's a ghost or not," I said. "It's . . . it's hard to explain."

The man nodded. "The spirit world is not easy," he said softly. "The spirits move in ways we cannot imagine. Wouldn't it be nice if we could just pick up the phone . . ."

He lifted the phone off his desk and raised it to his ear.

" . . . just pick up the phone, and call a certain number, and be in touch . . . in touch with the dead?"

I felt a chill run down my back. The phone he held—could it really reach ghosts? Something about the way he spoke made me believe that he really was in touch with spirits.

Or was I just getting carried away again?

"Sometimes ghosts don't speak at all," the man said. He kept the phone at his ear. His glasses gleamed in the light. The glare made it look as if his eyes were on fire.

"Sometimes they howl," he said, grinning at Vanessa and me. "Sometimes they howl out all the pain that is inside them."

I started to say something. But he tilted back his head and opened his mouth in a high, shrill howl.

"Let's go," Vanessa whispered, edging to the door. "I mean it, Spencer."

The little man laughed. "Sorry. Sometimes I just feel like howling. Does it ever happen to you?"

"Not really," I replied.

He set down the phone. Then he rubbed his hands together again. His hands were so flat and thin, they reminded me of butterfly wings.

"So what exactly are you looking for?" he asked. "A detector, right? You want to detect if ghosts are there or not."

"Well—" I started.

"No. We have to go," Vanessa interrupted. "We're late. We really can't spend any more time."

"I guess I have to go," I said. "Uh . . . maybe I'll come back some other time." Vanessa was already at the door. I took a few steps after her.

"I know what you need," the man said. "I have one here for you. It's exactly what you need."

I stopped and turned back to him. I knew I couldn't leave. I knew I had to see what he was talking about.

"Exactly what you need," he repeated in that deep voice. A tiny, frail man with such a deep, powerful voice. He curled his pointer finger, drawing me back, pulling me back to him.

"Spencer—don't!" Vanessa warned.

But I had to know. "What is it?" I asked.

He didn't answer. He moved to the dark display case and pulled something off a bottom shelf. Then he brought it into the light and held it up to me between his hands.

It was a square gray box with a yellow dial, a round speaker, and a red button on the front. It looked a lot like an ordinary radio.

"It's called the Howler," the man said.

I stepped up close and ran my hand over the dial. "What does it do?"

"It doesn't do anything," Vanessa chimed in from the front door. "Let's go. Don't waste any more of your money. You promised you wouldn't—remember?"

I gazed at the yellow dial. The round black speaker. I ran my hand over the top of the smooth gray case. "The Howler?" I repeated. "Why is it called that? What does it mean?"

"It's a kind of detector," the man replied, peering at me over his glasses. "It breaks down electrical sound waves. It detects the howls of ghosts."

"Whoa." I jerked my hand away from it.

"Spennn-cer!" Vanessa called.

"Does it summon ghosts?" I asked. "Does it—can it call to them?"

The man shook his head. "No. It doesn't summon ghosts. It only picks up their howls if they are already nearby."

He tilted the box up to me. "Then—see this red button? If you hear a ghost howling, you press this red button. And you speak into this black circle here. And you can talk to the ghost."

"The ghost will *hear* you?" I asked. "And he will answer back?"

"Only if he wants to answer," the man said. He lowered his face to mine and spoke in a whisper, "Sometimes the ghost is in such pain, he can only howl. He cannot speak."

"Can you *see* the ghost?" I asked.

The man shook his head. "The machine picks up only sound waves. Sound waves from the other side."

I swallowed. My heart was racing. I turned to Vanessa. "This is what I've been looking for," I said. "Do you believe it?"

She rolled her eyes. "No, I don't."

I ignored her. I knew I had to have the Howler. "How much is it?" I asked.

The man glanced down at the box in his hands, then back up to me. "How much would you like to pay?"

"Well . . . I have thirty dollars left over from Christmas presents," I told him.

He shut his eyes for a moment. "Okay," he said.

45

"Thirty dollars. I'll let you have this one cheap, since it's a floor model."

I pulled my wallet from my pants pocket. "Okay! I'll buy it," I said.

"Spencer . . ." Vanessa was still trying to stop me. "Remember the specter detector?"

The man snickered. "Do you have one of those? You didn't expect it to work, did you? That's just a toy. It's a kiddie thing."

I handed him my thirty dollars. He gently placed the Howler into my hands.

"Will this one work?" I asked.

The man's grin grew very wide. Once again, his face crinkled with a thousand tiny lines, and his eyeglasses appeared to light up.

"Oh, yes," he said. "It will work. It will work very well. But take one warning from someone who knows. . . . Ghosts are no longer entirely human. You may wish it *didn't* work."

I crept up the stairs to my room, keeping the Howler half hidden under the front of my coat. I could hear music coming from Nick's room. I didn't want him to see the Howler and start making fun of me before I even had a chance to try it out.

I set the little box down on my bed. Then I closed my bedroom door.

I moved my CD player and all my CDs off the little table next to my closet. Then I carefully set the Howler down and plugged it in.

Vanessa refused to come home with me to test it out. She kept warning me that this one wouldn't work either. "You just threw away your last thirty dollars," she said.

"Maybe you're right," I sighed. "But I want to believe. I really *want* to believe."

"Scott is right to tease you," she said.

That hurt. Wow, that hurt!

But here I was, up in my room, feeling really

47

excited. Nervous. About to test my new purchase.

I shut everything else out of my mind and pulled my desk chair in front of the table. Then I leaned over the Howler and gently wrapped my fingers around the power switch. I clicked it on.

The dial lit up instantly. It gave off a dim yellow glow.

I brought my face close to the speaker and listened.

Nothing. Silence.

I searched for a volume control, but I couldn't find one.

I stared at the dial. The yellow glow appeared to grow brighter.

I heard a buzz. A crackling sound, like static on the radio.

I pressed my ear to the speaker and listened for ghostly howls.

Nothing.

"Come on, ghosts," I said out loud. "Where are you?"

Give it a chance, I told myself.

I heard another crackle of static. The yellow dial flickered. Then silence.

How long did I sit there, staring at the yellow dial? Five minutes? Ten?

After a while, I stood up. I paced around the room. Then I crossed to the window and gazed down toward Scott's house.

He was just getting home. I saw him pause at his back door and look up at my window.

I ducked back so he wouldn't see me. I didn't want him barging in and giving me a hard time about the Howler. That's the last thing I wanted!

I turned back to the Howler, glowing and silent on my little table.

I sat back down in front of it. Leaned my elbows on the table. And stared into the dial.

Come on, I urged silently. Let me hear something. Just one tiny ghost sound.

I nearly fell off the chair when I heard a ghostly whisper.

"Spennnn-cerrrrr."

A spirit! A ghost! I could hear it! So close! It sounded so close!

"Spennnn-cerrrrr."

And then it grabbed me from behind.

And spun me around.

"Nick!" I cried. "You jerk! Let go of me!"

He giggled and gave me a hard shove that sent me sprawling over the table. Then he tossed my backpack to the floor and took its place on my bed.

"What's up, wimpface?"

"Nothing you'd be interested in," I sneered. "Would you please get out of my room? I'm kind of busy."

He spit his bubble gum toward the wastebasket in the corner—and missed. The gum bounced off the wall, onto my carpet.

"Hey, pick it up," I said.

He grinned at me. "Pick *what* up?" He jumped to his feet and came up behind me. "What's that thing? Another stupid ghost toy?"

"No, it's not a toy," I replied. But I was immediately sorry. I should have told Nick it was a toy, I thought. Then he'd go away and leave me alone.

Now I was going to have to explain.

He picked it up off the table. "Is it a radio?"

"Kind of," I said. "It's called the Howler. It uses radio waves or something. It picks up the howls of ghosts."

He snickered. "Yeah, sure." He raised the Howler to his ear.

"Careful—you'll unplug it," I warned.

Nick narrowed his eyes at me. "Are you becoming some kind of *Star Trek* freak? Is that what this is about?"

"No way," I said. "I just—"

He pressed his mouth against the dial. "Beam me up, Scotty!" he shouted into it. "Beam me up. This is Spock!"

He laughed really hard, as if he'd just made a really funny joke. Then he dropped the Howler to the table.

"Careful!" I screamed. "You'll break it."

He started to the door. "You're pitiful," he said. "It's not even funny, you're so totally pitiful. You really think you can buy some kind of stupid little radio and be able to hear ghosts howling."

"Just leave me alone!" I cried.

"Pitiful," he repeated. And he walked out of my room.

Pitiful. The word repeated in my ear.

Maybe he's right, I thought, staring at the silent gray box. Maybe I *am* pitiful.

• • •

Or maybe not.

Late that night, I was awakened by a strange sound.

I sat up in bed and listened.

The room was hot. The furnace had been on full blast. I was sweating, and my pajamas clung to my skin.

Pale, silvery moonlight poured into my room from the window. I blinked myself awake. Stretched my arms over my head. Turned toward the yellow glow of the Howler across my room.

What was that sound? What had awakened me?

Owoooooooooooooo.

A howl. So faint. So soft.

And then another. *Oooooooooowoooooo.*

Howls of pain. Ghostly howls . . . coming from the Howler.

I kicked the blankets off and struggled to my feet. My heart started to pound.

I reached for the lamp on my bed table and nearly knocked it over. Finally, I clicked on the light.

Oooooooooooowoo.

The howl sounded fainter now. Distant.

The yellow dial glowed.

I straightened my pajama pants and dove to the little table. I dropped into the chair, trembling with excitement.

And fear.

I grabbed the sides of the little box and listened.

Another howl, so sad, so far away.

My hands were suddenly cold and wet. I pressed them tighter against the sides of the Howler.

Was I really listening to a ghost? Was I really picking up sound from the spirit world?

This is what I had wanted. This is what I had dreamed about.

But now that it was actually happening, I was *terrified*.

My teeth started to chatter. I couldn't stop my body from shivering.

Ghosts are dead people, I thought. Dead people.

I heard another long, low howl pour out of the box.

Was I really listening to the cry of a dead person?

I stared at the box between my hands. At the yellow dial. At the red button beneath it. The red button . . .

In my excitement, I had completely forgotten. If I pushed the red button, I could talk to the ghost. I could communicate with it.

My hand trembled as I pressed the red button and held it down. I leaned closer to the box. "Hello," I called. My voice came out in a choked whisper.

"Hello?" I tried again.

Silence now. I waited, my heart thudding.

"Can anyone hear me?" I asked, holding the red button down.

Silence. A long, empty silence.

And then I heard a whispered voice. So soft, so far away, I could barely hear it. *"Please . . ."*

I let out a startled cry.

A voice from beyond!

"It's happening! It's real!"

I felt like leaping out of the chair and jumping up and down.

But instead, I pressed the red button and leaned

closer to the Howler. "I can hear you!" I cried. "It's working. I can hear you!"

I stared at the little round speaker and listened.

Silence. Only for a few seconds, but it seemed endless.

And then another whisper. *"Please . . . help."*

Help? How? Where was this ghost? Was he buried somewhere? Was he buried in a coffin deep in the ground?

I wanted to ask a million questions. But I was gasping for breath now. My heart pounded so hard, I couldn't breathe. Couldn't speak.

"Please help me. . . ." the voice whispered.

"Where are you?" I finally managed to choke out. "Who are you? How can I help?"

Silence.

I stood up. Then I sat back down. I tried to force my legs to stop shaking.

Behind me, the radiator rattled, sending more heat into the room. I knew my room was toasty warm. But I felt so cold. So cold down to my bones.

"Can you hear me?" I said into the box. "Who are you? Please answer. Who are you?"

Silence.

And then the whisper came again. *"Help me. . . ."*

"Who are you?" I demanded. "Where are you?"

"Buried . . ."

The word made me gasp.

Hugging myself to stop from shaking, I pressed

my ear to the speaker. And listened for more.

But once again the Howler was silent.

I pressed the red button. "How can I help you?" I asked. "What can I do? Who are you? Please—tell me."

Silence.

And then: *"Find me. Please—find me. . . ."*

"But where are you?" I asked. "Who are you?" I took a deep, shuddering breath. "Ian? Is it you? Ian?"

I shut my eyes and crossed my fingers.

Please—let it be him!

"Ian? Answer me. Is that you?" I whispered.

Silence now.

I waited. And waited. But the box had gone silent. The contact was lost.

Swallowing hard, I sat there, staring at the silent machine.

"Ghosts do exist," I murmured. "I heard one. I really heard one. Was it Ian? Does this mean I'll be able to contact Ian?"

I stood up. I stepped away from the chair and started to jump up and down. I couldn't control myself. I had to jump—for excitement, for fear, for the total shock of it.

I knew I'd never get back to sleep that night.

• • •

I wasn't going to tell Nick. But once we were sitting across from each other at the breakfast table in the kitchen, I couldn't hold it in.

"The Howler works," I whispered. Mom was at the sink, washing out the egg pan. "I heard a ghost last night. For real."

Nick chewed his cornflakes noisily. "You mean you had a bad dream," he said. He didn't look up from his cereal bowl.

"No. It wasn't a dream," I said. "A ghost was howling. It woke me up. And then he talked to me."

"Yeah, sure," Nick muttered.

"He sounded really far away, but I heard him so clearly," I said. "He talked to me."

Nick finally looked up from his bowl. "Did he tell you to brush your teeth? Your breath stinks."

"Nick—" I started.

Wiping her hands, Mom came over to the table. "What are you two talking about?" she asked.

"Spencer had a bad dream," Nick told her.

"No, I didn't!" I cried. "I—"

"It was about a ghost," Nick said. "It really got him scared."

"Mom, that's not true!" I insisted.

"Take it easy, Spencer," Mom said, patting my head gently. "I thought you were over those nightmares. Has anything been upsetting you lately?"

"Yeah. His face!" Nick cracked.

"Nick, give him a break," Mom said. "You can see he's upset."

"*I'm not upset!*" I screamed.

"Okay, okay," Mom said, raising her hands and backing away as if surrendering. "Let's talk about it later."

I choked down the rest of my scrambled eggs, glaring at Nick the whole time. Why did I waste my breath trying to tell Nick anything?

He thinks life is just a big joke. And always a joke at my expense.

Well, I didn't care what he thought. I had a machine that actually contacted ghosts. And maybe . . . maybe my long wait would soon be over. Maybe I'd be talking with my cousin Ian really soon.

At school, I told Vanessa all about it.

She stared at me for a long time. "You're serious? You didn't dream it or something?"

I groaned. "That's the same thing Nick said. But it happened, Vanessa. It really happened. The Howler works."

Her eyes went wide. "Wow. Do you think I could hear a ghost too?"

"Meet me after school," I said. "We can go to my house and try it. It's amazing!"

I met Vanessa behind the middle school parking lot after school. Ed and Justin, two guys from our class, were waiting with her.

Ed and Justin look as if they are brothers, but they're not. They're both tall and lanky. They both have straight brown hair cut pretty short, brown eyes, and long, serious faces.

They both wear baggy cargo pants with millions of pockets and zippers. They're both on the basketball team, and they both in-line skate to and from school every day. They even have the same laugh— a high-pitched horse whinny.

Everyone calls them the Twins, even though they're not related at all.

"Vanessa told us about your radio thing," Justin said. "Can we hear it too?"

"We won't make jokes or anything," Ed added. "Vanessa said you're really serious about this."

"Well . . . it's kind of scary," I replied. "You shouldn't come over if you're afraid of hearing dead people."

"They're doing a science project about haunted houses," Vanessa said. "They really want to hear a ghost."

I nodded. "Okay. Let's give it a try."

A few minutes later, I led them upstairs to my room. Nick was home. I heard the TV on in his bedroom down the hall. But his door was closed.

I ushered everyone inside and closed my door after them. They tossed their coats and backpacks on the bed. Then I sat down in front of the Howler, and they huddled around me.

I turned the knob and clicked it on. The yellow dial lit up.

"Cool," Justin said. "Can you get the rap station on this? Q-102?"

Ed gave him a shove. "Come on. We said no jokes."

"It's not a radio," I said. "It picks up sound waves. From the other side."

"The other side of what? The street?" Justin joked.

Ed laughed. Vanessa glared at them. "Shape up, guys. You promised."

"It isn't funny," I murmured, turning to concentrate on the Howler. "The ghosts are in a lot of pain. That's why they howl."

Ed tossed back his head and let out a long, loud howl. Justin joined in.

"Shhhh. Give it a rest," Vanessa said, leaning over my shoulder. "I think I just heard something."

Ed and Justin turned to the machine. All four of us stared at the glowing yellow dial and listened.

Silence.

From down the hall, I could hear Nick's TV. I prayed for him to stay in his room. I knew he'd love to burst in here and ruin everything.

"What's taking the ghosts so long?" Ed asked, bouncing up and down impatiently. "I've got a piano lesson at four."

"Shhhh. Give it a chance," I insisted.

"But it isn't making any noise at all," Vanessa said.

"I told you. Last night a ghost called to me. It was the scariest thing that ever happened to me," I said.

Ed let out a long sigh. He crossed to the window and sat down on the ledge. Justin backed away and dropped down on top of the coats on my bed.

Vanessa and I stared at the Howler.

Silence.

Silence.

And then . . .

Oooooooooowoooo.

An eerie howl. So soft. So faint.

But a howl. A frightening, shrill howl.

Ed and Justin were back on their feet.

"Oh, wow," Ed murmured, hurrying back to the table.

"What was that?" Justin asked in a whisper. "Did you hear it too?"

All four of us leaned close to the little gray box.

We heard another long, sad howl.

And then . . . then . . .

A raspy croak.

A ghostly voice, so frail, so chilling.

And the words, the terrifying words . . .

"*I see you. I can see all four of you. . . .*"

"No!" Vanessa uttered a cry and grabbed the back of my chair.

Ed and Justin huddled close, their mouths open, their eyes bulging.

My chest ached. I realized I'd been holding my breath the whole time. I let out a long whoosh of air.

"Is it a real ghost?" Justin asked in a whisper.

"Is it in this room with us?"

"I'll try to ask it," I said. I reached for the red button. But before I could push it, we heard the soft, croaking voice again: *"I see you . . . You must help . . . Help me."*

Justin squeezed my shoulder. "Spencer, this is too freaky," he said. "I—I don't even believe in ghosts."

"I think I believe now!" Vanessa whispered.

"Owoooooooooooooooo." The howl sounded closer this time. Angrier.

I felt a chill on the back of my neck, as if the ghost were breathing on me.

I whipped around, expecting to see a ghostly figure. But no. Only my friends leaning over me, staring at the Howler.

I took a deep breath. Then I reached out and pressed the red button. "We . . . we can hear you," I stammered. "Are you here? Are you here in this room?"

Silence.

And then another low howl. *"Help me. . . . Please help me. . . ."*

"How?" I shouted into the speaker. "How can we help you? Where are you?"

"I've been . . . buried . . . buried . . . so long."

I turned and saw Justin backing out of the room. "This is way creepy," he said. "I—I think I have to go now."

"Shhh. Don't go," Vanessa whispered. "Let's see what the ghost wants."

"Wh-what if he wants to make us ghosts too?" Justin cried. He had backed all the way to the door.

"Is he here?" Ed asked breathlessly. "Is he really here?" He seemed to be in shock or something. His eyes kept darting back and forth. He had grown very pale.

I turned back to the Howler and pressed the red button. "Where are you?" I demanded, speaking into the box.

"Help me. . . . Help me. . . ." the voice rasped. *"I'm buried . . . buried in your closet."*

"NO!" I gasped.

Vanessa squeezed my shoulder so hard, it hurt. Ed and Justin stood frozen like statues.

"*In your closet . . .*" the ghost repeated. "*Help me—please! I've been buried . . . so long. . . . Let me out! Let me out!*"

I jumped to my feet.

"Wh-what are you doing?" Vanessa demanded, her face tight with fear.

I pointed to the closet beside the little table. "I'm going to open it. We have to see—"

"No!" Justin and Ed screamed together. "Spencer, don't do it!"

Vanessa raised her hands to the sides of her face. She stared at the closet and didn't say anything.

"It's—it's in there," Ed said in a trembling voice. "Don't go there, Spencer. Don't open the door."

"I have to," I said. I reached for the doorknob.

Ed and Justin had both backed to the attic door. Vanessa stood in the middle of the room, hands still pressed to her face. "Go ahead," she whispered. "You know you're going to do it. So go ahead. Open the door."

I squeezed the knob. Turned it.

And jerked open the closet door.

"AAAAAAGGGH!"

Shrieking at the top of his lungs, the ghost came bursting out of the closet.

Only it wasn't a ghost. It was my brother, Nick.

I let out a scream. We all screamed. Ed fell back against the wall.

And Nick started laughing. He grabbed me and spun me around. He danced gleefully around the room. He shoved away the coats and jumped up and down on the bed.

"You bozos!" he cried. "You bozos! Couldn't you tell it was me? Couldn't you tell the voice was coming from the closet?"

Vanessa sank onto the desk chair. She shook her head, her eyes lowered to the floor.

"You bozos!" Nick cried. He pumped his fists over his head as if celebrating a great victory. "You bozos!"

"I knew it wasn't real," Justin muttered. "I knew it wasn't a ghost."

"Liar," Ed said, giving him a shove. "You were shaking even more than me."

I wanted to scream, but I was speechless. I had never been so disappointed in my life.

"I'm buried . . . buried in your closet," Nick rasped. Then he laughed his head off some more. "I heard you guys coming up the stairs. I knew why you were here. I knew Spencer wanted to show off his new toy. So I ran to the closet. I knew you would fall for my little joke."

"That was mean," Vanessa murmured, her head still down.

"Mean—and funny!" Nick exclaimed.

I turned to Nick. I wanted to tackle him. Bring him down to the floor. And punch him and punch him and punch him.

"Was that you I heard last night?" I asked. "Was that you playing the same trick on me?"

A grin spread over Nick's face. He nodded. "Three guesses." He crossed the room and smacked the top of the Howler. "Your machine is a fake, Spencer. Take it back to the store. Admit you were a jerk."

I stared at the Howler and sighed. Another worthless piece of junk.

Nick trotted to his room, still chuckling merrily to himself. I slammed the door behind him and turned to my friends.

They had sprawled on the floor. The closet door stood open. The dial on the Howler glowed brightly.

The speaker crackled with static.

Vanessa had a strange smile on her face. "What's so funny?" I muttered.

"I just had an idea," she replied. Her grin grew wider. "An awesome idea."

I slumped onto the edge of the bed and let out another unhappy sigh. "What is it?"

"Your brother's trick was mean," Vanessa said. "But it's a really good trick. What if we play it on Scott?"

"Yesss!" Justin and Ed cried out together. They slapped each other a high-five.

I wasn't in the mood for playing tricks. "Why should we?" I asked.

"He played that mean trick on you with the clothing dummy," Vanessa replied. "And then he told everyone in school how he fooled you and made you scream."

"And he's been lying for months about how his house is haunted," Ed chimed in.

"So what if we play this trick and make Scott think his house really *is* haunted?" Vanessa continued. "He'll freak. He'll totally freak!"

"Whoa! And once we tell everyone, he'll never be able to brag again!" Ed exclaimed.

They turned to me, waiting for my reaction.

"I didn't buy the Howler just to play tricks with it," I said sadly.

Vanessa put a hand on my shoulder. "But wouldn't

it cheer you up to fool Scott and scare him out of his mind?"

I couldn't hold back a smile. "Well . . . maybe a little," I said. "Let's do it!"

On Monday, Vanessa, Ed, and Justin met at my house after school. I had the Howler ready to go. I just wanted to talk over the plan to scare Scott.

"Vanessa, Ed, and I will go in through Scott's back door. We'll make sure the door isn't locked, so Justin can sneak in later. Then we'll keep Scott busy in the living room or in his room, so he doesn't see Justin come in."

"And where do I go?" Justin asked. "Up to the attic?"

I nodded. "Yes, you sneak up to the attic. It's a big L-shaped room. You'll see a closet just before the room turns. You hide in that closet."

"Then we bring Scott up to the attic and set up the Howler next to the closet where Justin is hiding," Vanessa said.

"Cool," Ed said, grinning. "This is totally cool."

I chuckled. "I'm so sick of Scott bragging about how his house is haunted. I can't wait to see what he does when he thinks he's hearing a *real* ghost!"

"He'll die!" Vanessa exclaimed, grinning. "He'll just die!"

"What's up, guys?" Scott greeted us at his kitchen door. He had a half-eaten brownie in his hand and chocolate smeared on his chin.

"Do you have any more of those?" Ed asked, pointing at the brownie. "I'm starving."

Scott shoved the rest of the brownie into his mouth. "That's the last one," he said, chewing hard.

The three of us stepped into the kitchen. "How come you weren't in school today?" Vanessa asked him.

"I had a bad stomachache this morning," he said.

Probably from eating too many brownies, I thought.

"I brought something you might be interested in," I told Scott. I held up the Howler.

Scott wiped his chocolaty fingers off on the legs of his jeans. He took the Howler from me and examined it. "What does it do? Didn't you have another one of these in your room last week?"

"This one is different," I said. "This one works."

"We saw it work," Ed said. "It's no joke."

"But what does it do?" Scott asked, turning the box over in his hands.

"It's called the Howler," I said. "Can we sit down somewhere? I'll explain it to you."

Scott led the way to the small den on the other side of the living room. I hung back in the kitchen for just a second. I pulled the back door open just a crack so that Justin could slip in.

Then I hurried to catch up to the others. As I made my way across the kitchen, I saw a plate on the counter stacked high with brownies.

What a liar, I thought. He wanted to save them all for himself.

We tossed off our coats and threw them on the den floor. Then we sat around on the green leather furniture, and I explained the Howler to Scott.

At first, he laughed. "You've been watching too many cartoons."

"But we heard ghosts howling," Vanessa insisted. "It was really creepy, Scott. We heard a ghost, howling and begging us for help."

"I heard it too," Ed said. "It—it gave me nightmares last night."

Scott's grin faded.

Behind me, I heard the front stairs creak. I knew Justin was making his way up to the attic. We had to keep Scott talking a little while longer and give Justin time to get settled in the closet.

Scott studied the little gray box. "It picks up howls? And you can hear the ghosts talk?"

"You can talk to them too," I said. "You just push this red button and speak into that circle."

"Your house is haunted, right?" Vanessa said. "That's what you've been telling everyone. You've seen the ghosts walking around. So the Howler should work right away."

Scott hesitated. His mouth started to twitch nervously. "Well . . . I don't know. My ghosts don't come out in the daytime. Only at night."

He's looking for an excuse, I thought. He doesn't want us to use the Howler here. Because he doesn't want us to prove that there are no ghosts in this house.

"Maybe you can't see them in the daytime," I said. "But with the Howler, we can hear them."

"No. I don't think so," Scott insisted. "I don't want to bother them with that thing. You know. Why get them stirred up?"

"It won't bother them," I replied. "It—"

"Besides, I have too much homework," Scott said. "You guys should go. I really have to get started on it."

"But you weren't in school today," Vanessa said. "You don't have the homework assignments."

Scott started to look desperate. His mouth was twitching, and his face was bright red. He really didn't want us to prove what a fake he was.

I jumped to my feet and started to carry the Howler to the stairs. "Come on. Let's take it up to the attic and listen to these ghosts of yours."

Scott hurried to block my way. "Uh . . . that thing—it's not really real—right? It's a toy, like the other junk you bought?"

"I told you, this one works," I said. "You'll be surprised. I think you'll *really* be surprised."

Carrying the Howler in front of me, I led the way up the stairs. Scott pulled down the door in the ceiling, and we marched up to the attic.

The afternoon sun was lowering in the sky. Pale light washed in from the single window. Long shadows stretched across the cluttered floor.

"Wow. Nice attic," Ed said, glancing around. "It looks kind of haunted."

Scott didn't say anything.

I made my way across the room. "There's a plug over by the closet," I said. "We can plug the Howler in there."

Vanessa pulled a carton up beside the closet, and I set the box down on it. Then I reached behind the carton to plug the Howler in.

I squatted down on the floor in front of it and clicked it on. Vanessa, Ed, and Scott huddled behind me.

I glanced behind me and caught the tense expression on Scott's face.

I was enjoying our little joke already, even though it was just beginning. As I stared at the yellow dial, it was all I could do to keep from bursting out laughing.

Vanessa and Ed were also having trouble keeping straight faces. I could see they were really enjoying our little joke too.

"What's happening?" Scott asked nervously. "Is it on? What does it do now?"

"It's warming up," I replied. "You just have to wait and listen carefully. If there are any ghosts nearby, and if they're making any sounds, the Howler will pick them up."

"But—maybe my ghosts are silent," Scott said. "Maybe they don't howl. I think they probably sleep during the day."

"Do ghosts sleep?" Ed asked. "They're not alive, right? So why do they have to sleep?"

"Shhh." I raised a finger to my lips. I leaned closer to the gray box.

"I—I think I hear something," Vanessa said loudly.

That was Justin's cue to start making ghost sounds from the closet.

We all grew silent. Somewhere down the block, a car was honking its horn. The only other sounds were Scott's wheezing, rapid breaths right behind me.

A few seconds went by. We huddled there in front of the little machine, frozen, staring straight ahead, listening. And then . . .

Owoooooooooooo.

Soft. So very faint. Almost like a breath.

Scott gasped. "Did you hear that?"

I nodded solemnly. "The Howler is picking up something." I raised my finger to my lips again.

Vanessa dropped to her knees beside me. "Wow," she muttered, pretending to be amazed. She and I exchanged glances.

Ooooooooowooooo. Another howl, louder this time.

"The ghost seems so sad," I whispered. I turned to Scott. "That's why they howl. They can't stand the pain."

He nodded but didn't say anything. His eyes were bulging. His mouth kept twitching.

"I . . . I don't believe this!" Ed whispered.

"Help us . . . Help us out of here. . . ."

The raspy, whispered words made Scott cry out. "Turn it off!" he shrieked. "I—I don't want to disturb them!"

"Shhhh. Listen," I said, pointing to the speaker.

I pressed the red button. "Where are you?" I asked. "Are you in this room with us?"

Silence. A long, tense silence.

"Help us. . . . The snow is so high. . . ."

Vanessa covered her mouth. I could see she was about to laugh.

I turned and saw that Scott wasn't laughing. He was buying it.

He believed he was hearing a real ghost.

I pressed the red button. "Can you hear me?" I asked. "Where are you? Who are you? Please—tell us."

"The snow is so high," came the whisper. *"We've been snowed in for days. And we're so hungry . . . so hungry."*

"But where are you?" I called into the Howler. I turned to the others. "I don't think he can hear me."

"Maybe he's very far away," Scott said. He kept swallowing. He shoved his hands into his jeans pockets and stared at the gray box.

"Can you help us?" came the whisper. *"We've been trapped here for so long. We'd be so happy . . . so grateful. . . . Please . . ."*

I pressed my face close to the Howler. "We can help you," I said. "You have to tell us where you are."

"But—maybe we don't want to help them," Scott said softly.

Ed laughed. "You're chicken—aren't you!"

Scott didn't reply.

"The ghost sounds so sad," Vanessa said. "We have to help him."

"Please . . . let us out of here. Let us out!" came the cry, so faint, so far away.

Justin is doing an awesome job, I thought. Look at Scott. He's shaking like a leaf. Excellent! This is excellent!

I pressed the red button. "We will try to help

you," I shouted. "But you have to tell us where you are."

"In the closet," came the reply. *"Please . . . we've been in the closet for so long. . . . It's so dark, so cold. And we're very hungry. Please . . ."*

I jumped to my feet and turned to the closet.

This was the big moment. Time for Scott to get the scare of his life.

My heart was pounding. I couldn't wait. I caught the excited expressions on Vanessa's and Ed's faces.

"Wait—" Scott cried. "Spencer, where are you going?"

"To the closet," I said, pointing. "We have to open the closet."

"But—but—" Scott sputtered.

"You've told us all about the ghosts in this house," Vanessa said. "Don't you want to see them?"

"Don't you want to help them?" Ed added.

I didn't wait for Scott to answer. I pushed him up to the closet door. "Open it," I said.

He tried to back away, but we had him surrounded. He was trembling. Large beads of sweat rolled down the sides of his face.

"Open it, Scott," Vanessa urged.

"Just open it," I said.

"Okay, okay," he muttered. He grabbed the door handle. He took a deep breath.

Vanessa, Ed, and I braced ourselves. We were ready for the big moment.

79

Scott hesitated . . . hesitated. . . . Then he pulled open the closet door.

All four of us stared—stared into the shallow, dark closet.

THERE WAS NO ONE INSIDE.

"Oh, wow." I stared into the empty closet.

Vanessa grabbed my arm. "Where's Justin?" she whispered.

Before I could answer, I heard a clumping sound on the stairs. I turned and saw Justin step up into the attic.

"Hey, guys—sorry I'm late," he called. "My mom beeped me, and I had to see what it was about."

Scott still had his hand on the closet doorknob. He turned to me, his expression puzzled. "What's going on, Spencer?"

Ed's eyes were wide with fear. "I—I don't get it," he murmured.

"Ohhhhh!" I let out a startled cry as a blast of freezing air shot out of the closet.

Scott's hand flew off the door handle, and he stumbled back. Another powerful blast sent Vanessa, Ed, and me staggering back across the attic.

"Ohhh, the smell!" I moaned. The cold air smelled like rotting meat.

Justin had stopped in the middle of the room. "What's up?" he called. "Did you start without me?"

And then his expression changed, and he started to gag as the cold, putrid air swirled around him.

"Shut the door!" Scott shouted. "Hurry! Shut the closet door!"

I pinched two fingers over my nose to keep the disgusting odor out. Then I lowered my head into the swirling wind and took a few steps toward the closet.

But a high, shrill scream made me stop.

The scream rose up from the closet like a police siren. And rose and rose—until it became a deafening screech.

My eardrums felt about to burst. I slapped my hands over my ears. But I couldn't keep out the horrifying, painfully shrill wail.

Holding my head, I struggled toward the closet. But the putrid wind swirled, pushing me back . . . back.

I stumbled. Fell to my knees. The wind raged over me.

And over its howl, I heard voices. Chattering, excited whispers.

"Free . . ."

"We are free. . . . At last we have been set free!"

"Make them pay! Make them pay!"

I raised my head and saw Vanessa down on her knees too. Bent under the rushing blasts of wind.

Ed lay flat on the floor. He didn't move.

Scott hunched in a corner, holding his head.

Another siren cry tore through me. The crushing pain shot over me. Violent streaks of yellow lightning exploded across the attic. I shut my eyes tight but couldn't close out the blinding light.

When I opened my eyes, I saw Justin bent over, puking his guts out near the stairs. Vanessa sprawled facedown on the floor, her head buried beneath her hands.

The sickening wind spun around us. Held us in place.

The raspy, ugly voices hissed and whispered and laughed. And another long, high shriek made me cry out in agony.

"Oh, no!" I wailed. "What have we done? What have we done?"

"Pay them back! Pay them back!"

The voices rasped on the swirling, freezing winds.

"A hundred years—but now we're FREE!"

I uttered a terrified moan. My stomach churned from the thick, sour odor. Pushing against the wind, I forced myself to my feet.

Shut the closet door.

I've got to shut the door.

The howling wind roared over me. I lowered my shoulder into it. I shut my eyes. And pushed forward with all my strength.

Pushed . . .

It felt as if I were trying to shove my way through a solid wall.

The thick, sour odor made my stomach churn. I held my breath, but I couldn't shut out the smell.

One step forward . . . another . . .

I can't get there, I realized. The wind is too strong.

Can't . . . can't . . .

"Ohhhh!" I cried out as I fell. Fell forward.

I staggered into the closet door. Raised both hands—and slammed it shut.

Yes!

The roaring wind stopped. Silence now. A heavy, eerie silence. The sour smell lingered in my nose. I could taste it when I swallowed.

I blinked, gazing at the closet door, feeling dizzy and dazed.

Did I do it? Did I lock those ghosts in?

The room spinning, I turned to my friends. "Hurry! We've got to get out of here!"

I grabbed Vanessa's hand and tried to pull her to her feet. "Come on! Move!" I dragged her up. I pulled her toward the attic stairs.

Justin sat up, shaking his head, blinking, looking very confused. Ed lay beside him, on his back on the floor, groaning, holding his stomach.

"Hurry!" I shouted. "Get downstairs! We've got to get away from here!"

I pulled Vanessa another few steps, stumbling over small cartons and piles of newspapers. Scott was already running down the stairs. Vanessa and I followed close behind him.

"Hurry!" I shouted up to Ed and Justin. "Move!"

They came stumbling down the stairs. Scott grabbed the ceiling door with both hands. He hoisted it to the ceiling and shoved the metal bolt shut.

Panting like animals, we huddled on the floor. I

could still hear the siren howls ringing in my ears. The putrid smell of death, of decay, clung to my skin and my clothes.

"L-let's go," I stammered. I started toward the front door.

"Don't leave me here!" Scott tugged me back. "I— I didn't know," he said. "I didn't know there were real ghosts up there, Spencer. I made up all the stories."

I raised my eyes to the ceiling door. "It's okay," I said. "It's quiet now. We locked them in. We locked them back in the closet. You'll be okay."

Scott's chin was trembling. Beads of sweat rolled down his forehead. "I'm never going up there again. Never!" he said.

"I've tried to contact ghosts for a year. I had no idea it would be so terrifying. I'm never going to try again," I declared. "Never."

Little did I realize that I'd be risking my life back in Scott's attic a few days later.

The next few days whirred past in a blur. I was in a total daze. I couldn't shut the ghosts from my mind.

Will I ever forget that terrifying scene? I wondered.

I couldn't concentrate on my schoolwork. I could barely think straight!

After school on Tuesday, I was down on the floor of my room, frantically painting a poster. The poster was due on Wednesday. I had completely forgotten I'd entered the school poster art contest.

I knew that most kids would be doing a lot of fancy graphics on their computers. I decided to do my poster the old-fashioned way.

I had cans of red and black paint and three different-sized brushes spread out on the floor beside my sheet of poster board. I planned to write "ROAR, TIGERS!" in bold black letters at the top. Tigers is the name of our school sports teams.

I had already sketched a very angry, roaring tiger head in pencil. I planned to give it red-and-black stripes. Make it really jump off the poster.

Leaning over the poster board, I had just started to paint the black outline of the head, when I heard footsteps. And someone calling me.

I glanced up to see Scott step into my room. I hadn't seen him in school that day. But I really didn't have time to talk.

"Hey, Spencer—" He stopped a few inches from the poster. "You're still working on your poster? I finished mine last week. I did some really cool things on my computer."

"I forgot all about the poster contest," I said. "So now I'm in a rush." I didn't look up. I kept moving the brush, filling in my sketch.

"Is that a dog?" Scott asked.

I groaned. "No. A tiger." I dropped the brush onto the newspaper I'd spread. "What's up, Scott? Are you okay? Have you seen any ghosts?"

His smile faded. He shook his head. "No. It's been quiet. I think we locked them up."

"Good," I muttered. A chill ran down my back, thinking about those ghosts.

"I told my parents the whole story," Scott said. "I told them everything."

"And what did they say?" I asked.

He frowned. "They told me to save the ghost stories for Halloween."

My mouth dropped open. "You mean . . . they didn't believe you?"

He shook his head. "No. They didn't. And there was *no way* I'd take them up to the attic and open the closet door to prove it to them."

"Good move," I said. I knew his parents wouldn't believe him. My parents wouldn't believe it either. I guess that's why I didn't tell them about it.

"I'm still kind of scared," Scott admitted. "I jump every time I hear a creak or any noise. I think those ghosts are going to come jumping out at me."

I nodded my head. "I know what you mean. I've been thinking about them too. But I think we locked them up. You're safe as long as no one opens that closet."

I could see him thinking hard about that. A few minutes later, he left. I grabbed my paintbrush, leaned over the poster, and went back to work.

"What's that mess you're making, punk?" Nick came bursting into my room a few minutes later.

"I have to paint a poster," I said.

"A poster? It looks more like you puked up your lunch."

"Thanks, Nick. You're a nice guy," I said.

He moved closer until he blocked out the light. I couldn't see what I was painting.

"What does 'I' stand for?" he asked.

"'I'?"

"Yeah. 'I,'" he repeated. "What does it stand for?"

I thought hard. "Uh . . . idiot?"

"At least you know your name," Nick said, grinning. "But you got it wrong. 'I' stands for ice cream."

I rolled my eyes. "Why are you telling me this?" I asked.

"Because we don't have any good ice cream in the freezer." He nudged me softly in the side with one of his big boots. "Get going, punk. Buy two pints, okay? Use your own money. I'm a little broke this week."

"No way, Nick!" I shouted. "I'm not doing it! I'm not!"

"Hurry back," Nick said. "It's almost dinnertime. You don't want to be late."

"No!" I shouted. "No! No! NO!"

He raised his boot and held it over my poster. "Do you think your poster will look better before or after I step on it?" He started to lower the boot.

"No! No way!" I insisted. I shoved his foot away. "I have to get this poster done! I'm not going for ice cream, Nick! Now, beat it! BEAT IT!"

He backed up a step. "Okay, okay," he muttered. "Don't have a hissy fit." To my surprise, he turned and stomped out of the room.

"Wow! I won!" I exclaimed.

What a victory! I had never stood up to Nick before. Never. And the first time I did—I won!

I leaned over the poster and started to paint again.

But I didn't have long to paint. A few minutes later, I heard Mom calling from downstairs. "Spencer, your dad is back from the supermarket. Come help him put away the groceries."

"But, Mom, I'm busy," I protested. "Why can't Nick do it this week?"

"Because it's your job!" Mom shouted. "Hurry. I've almost got dinner ready."

I had no choice. I dropped the paintbrush into the can of red paint and hurried downstairs to help my dad.

It didn't take long. I set the world record for emptying shopping bags. Then I hurried back upstairs.

I stepped into my room—and let out a sharp cry. "Oh, NO!"

A thick red stripe. Someone had painted a thick red stripe down my bedroom wall.

No. Not a stripe.

The letter I! A long red I!

"NICK! YOU JERK!" I screamed. "YOU JERK! YOU JERK!"

"Huh? What's your problem?" Nick stepped out of his room. He waved the phone in his hand. "Can't you see I'm on the phone?"

"You jerk!" I shrieked. "How could you do that? How could you ruin my whole wall?"

"I don't know what you're babbling about," Nick said. "Go back in your cage, okay?"

"No!" I screamed. "It's not okay!" I ran down the hall and grabbed him by the arm. "Come on! I'm telling Mom and Dad!"

Nick brushed me away. He raised the phone to his ear. "I'll have to call you back," he said into it. "My little brother is freaking out."

"What's going on?" Dad called. He and Mom appeared at the top of the stairs. Mom was carrying a blue suit on a hanger.

"He ruined my room!" I wailed. "He painted my wall!"

"He *what*?" Mom shrieked.

She and Dad hurried into my room. I heard their cries of shock and horror.

"Nick—get in here!" Dad growled.

Nick rolled his eyes. "What's up with all of you?" he muttered. He pushed me out of the way and strode into my room.

"Wow!" he exclaimed. "Spencer—you missed the paper by a mile!"

I stood in the doorway, my legs trembling. My heart pounded. "You know I didn't do it!" I told Nick. "*You* did it! You!"

"Nick—how could you vandalize your own brother's room?" Dad demanded angrily.

"I—I don't believe it," Mom sighed. "I feel sick just looking at it. I really do."

"But I didn't do it!" Nick cried. He raised his right hand. "I swear. I swear I didn't do it. I was in my room. I've been on my phone the whole time."

"Liar! There's no one else here," I said. "It had to be you."

"I know what you did, punk," Nick shouted. "You did it yourself. So that you could blame me and get me in trouble."

"Liar!" I screamed. I dove at Nick and tried to knock him over.

Dad had to separate us. "All of this shouting isn't getting us anywhere," he said. "Maybe the paint is washable. Maybe we can do something about it."

"Later. After dinner," Mom said. She dropped the

suit she was carrying onto my bed. "Try this on after dinner, Spencer. It's the suit you wore to my cousin's wedding. I had it let out. See if it fits."

"Try not to paint it red!" Nick said.

"Shut up!" I screamed. "You liar! Just because I didn't get your stupid ice cream!"

"Stop it—both of you," Dad ordered. "Let's try to have a quiet, civilized dinner—okay?"

"It's okay with me," I muttered.

But dinner didn't turn out too well.

"I know no one feels like eating after that disaster upstairs. But I made your favorite tonight," Mom said, setting the pan down in front of me on the kitchen table.

"Mmmm. Macaroni and cheese. It's *my* favorite too!" Dad declared.

I actually don't like macaroni very much. It's kind of boring. And I hate the way the cheese sticks to my teeth. But I've never had the nerve to admit it to Mom.

I glared across the table at my brother. He painted the wall, and he's going to get away with it, I realized. He's such a good liar. Mom and Dad believe him.

But he had to be the one who painted the wall. There's no one else in the house.

Mom spooned a big hunk of macaroni onto my plate. She piled up some green salad next to it.

I was just starting to eat, when I heard the whispers.

I turned in my chair. But there was no one there.

"Here . . . Here . . ."

That's what it sounded like.

I put my little finger in my ear and moved it around. I thought maybe I had wax stuck in there or something.

Across the table, Mom and Dad were talking about buying a new furnace. "The heating oil is costing a fortune," Dad said, spooning more salad onto his plate.

I started to eat again. But the whispers made me stop.

"Here. Over here . . ."

"Look up. Here."

I had a sudden sick feeling in the pit of my stomach. This isn't happening, I thought.

I turned around. My eyes searched the kitchen. No one there.

"Over here. Look here."

The ghosts? The ghosts from Scott's house?

Maybe we didn't lock them in the attic closet after all. Maybe they followed me home.

Maybe Nick was telling the truth. Maybe he didn't paint my wall. Maybe the ghosts painted it.

"But that's crazy." I didn't realize I had said it out loud.

"What's crazy?" Dad asked.

He and Mom were both staring hard at me.

"Oh. Sorry. I was thinking about something," I said.

"Here. Look up. Look here."

I felt a hot puff of air on the back of my neck. Like someone breathing.

I spun around. No one there.

"Look here."

Another hot puff of breath made my skin prickle.

"NOOOO!" I screamed. "Go away! Go away!"

I jumped to my feet. I knocked my glass over. It fell and cracked my dinner plate. Macaroni spilled onto the table, onto the floor.

"Here. Here. Look."

"NOOOO!" I shrieked again.

"Spencer—what's wrong?" Mom cried. She and Dad jumped up too.

"Don't you hear it?" I wailed. "Don't you hear it?"

"Hear *what*?" Dad cried.

I spun away from the table. The chair toppled over. But I didn't stop to pick it up.

I ran out of the kitchen. Up to my room. I slammed the door and locked it. But I knew that wouldn't keep them out.

The ghosts from Scott's attic had followed me, I knew.

Why were they here? And what did they plan to do now? Haunt me forever?

I called Scott. I told him about the red paint smear on my wall. And the frightening whispers at dinner.

He got very quiet.

"I think it might be the ghosts," I said. "Maybe we didn't lock that closet in time."

A long silence. "Everything is okay at my house," he said finally. "Totally normal."

Did the ghosts all move to *my* house? I wondered.

Later, I couldn't get to sleep. I lay in bed and stared across my dark room, wide awake. I listened for whispers. My eyes kept searching the shadows for signs of the ghosts.

I was finally drifting to sleep, when something caught my eye.

Something moved.

I blinked myself wide awake. I sat up quickly.

And saw the sleeve of my suit jacket move.

The suit Mom wanted me to try on. I had forgotten

about it. I had tossed it on the chair against the wall.

And now, as I gaped in silent horror, the sleeve raised itself. And then the other sleeve moved. And then the whole jacket floated up off the chair.

"Who's there?" I called. "Who is it?"

Silence.

I wanted to jump out of bed, but my legs wouldn't move. My whole body was frozen in fear.

"Hey—" I called out as the pants slowly lifted off the chair. One leg bent and lifted up. Then the other leg.

It looked as if someone was pulling on the pants.

Someone invisible.

"No—go away!" I cried, my voice choked with terror.

The suit—the jacket above the pants—floated a few inches above the floor. And then it began to move toward me.

With no one inside!

"N-noooo!" I let out another cry.

I struggled to climb out of bed. But the covers tangled around my legs. I kicked frantically as the suit floated closer.

Both jacket arms rose, as if preparing to grab me.

I finally managed to kick free of the covers. I leaped out of bed.

A cold wind swirled up from out of nowhere. The wind circled me, spun around me. The window shade began to flap. *Snap snap snap.* It flapped hard against the bedroom window.

The window slid up, then slammed back down. It shot up again, opening all the way. Then an invisible hand sent it slamming down.

Arms raised, the suit floated closer . . . closer. . . .

And I opened my mouth in a shrill scream of terror.

"Spencer—what's wrong?"

"What's happening?"

The ceiling light flashed on. Mom and Dad burst in. Mom was wearing a long brown-and-white night-shirt. Dad was struggling with his bathrobe.

"We heard you scream," Dad said. "What—"

"The suit—" I choked out, pointing.

I gasped. The jacket and pants had settled back onto the chair.

"The suit was moving!" I said. "And the window started to shoot up and down."

Their eyes moved from the suit on the chair to the closed bedroom window.

Mom stepped up to me and placed a hand on my forehead. "Spencer, you're sweating. Your forehead is dripping wet. Do you have fever?"

"Were you having a nightmare?" Dad asked, star-ing at the suit lying so still over the chair.

"Someone was in the suit," I insisted. "Someone put it on and—"

Mom shook her head sadly. She still had her hand on my forehead. She lowered it around my shoulders. "I think something has upset you," she whispered.

"First he goes nuts at dinner. Now this," Dad muttered.

"Do you think we should take you to see Dr. Rausch?" Mom asked.

"No," I said. "I'm okay. It really happened. The suit—"

Mom and Dad exchanged glances. I could see they were worried about me.

And I could see they weren't going to believe me.

"I guess it *was* a nightmare," I said, lowering my eyes to the floor. "That's all. Just a nightmare."

That seemed to make them happy. Mom tucked me back into bed. Dad ran to get me a drink of water.

A few minutes later, they returned to their room.

I sat up in bed, thinking hard. Thinking about the suit . . . the whispers. . . .

Thinking about the ghosts from Scott's house.

And then I slapped my forehead. "I've been so stupid!" I cried out loud. "I've been so totally stupid!"

"Don't you understand? Don't you see how stupid I've been?" I asked.

Vanessa frowned. Justin and Ed shook their heads.

I'd invited them over after school. I knew they wouldn't like what I had planned. But I needed their help. I couldn't do it alone.

"The Howler," I said. "I forgot all about the Howler."

I pointed out the window. "It's still up in Scott's attic. I left it there. I was so scared of the ghosts. We all were so scared . . . I forgot about it. But now we have to get it back."

Vanessa gazed out at Scott's house through the bedroom window. "Go back up there?"

"You're kidding—right?" Ed said. "Remember we said we'd never go near Scott's attic again?"

"Remember what happened when we opened the closet door?" Justin added.

"Of course I remember," I said. "But those ghosts are gone now. They aren't up in Scott's attic anymore. They're in *my* house."

They all gasped and started to ask a million questions. So I told them everything that had happened. The paint smears. The whispers at dinner. The suit rising up in the darkness.

"Weird," Ed muttered.

"Aren't you scared?" Justin asked.

"Terrified," I replied. "But it's all worth it if I can reach Ian."

Vanessa's eyes burned into mine. "That's why you want to go back to Scott's attic? That's why you want to bring the Howler down?"

I nodded. "I've been driving myself crazy for a year, trying *everything* to reach my cousin. And the Howler has been sitting up there for days."

"Do you think you can reach Ian with it?" Ed asked.

"I have to try," I said.

I started to the door. "So—let's go," I said. "Who's coming with me?"

They didn't move.

"Don't all volunteer at once," I said. "Come on. I have to get it back. And I don't want to go alone. It's perfectly safe. It's safer in that attic than it is in my room."

"Do you really think so?" Vanessa asked.

"I'm sure of it," I said.

Scott greeted us at his kitchen door. He appeared very surprised to see us. And when I told him why we came, he was even more surprised.

He scratched his thick nest of black hair. "You really want to go back to the attic? What about the ghosts?"

"They're not up there anymore," I said. "I told you the other night—they moved to my house. I just want to get the Howler and take it home."

Scott snickered at me. "If you're not afraid of the ghosts up there, Spencer, why did you bring three friends?"

"Okay, okay. I was afraid to do it alone," I admitted. "I thought it would be safer if a bunch of us went up there."

"My parents aren't home," Scott said. "If something bad happens . . ."

"I'm just going to grab the Howler and get out of here," I said. "Nothing bad will happen."

Scott shrugged. "Whatever." He led the way up the stairs.

I helped him pull down the attic trapdoor. He jumped back behind Ed and Justin. "I'm not going first," he said.

"No problem," I said. "The ghosts aren't up there. You'll see." I started up the stairs.

My three friends followed. Scott climbed up last.

I gazed around the attic. Afternoon sunlight washed in through the dust-smeared window. Where the sunlight ended, deep shadows spread over the room.

I could see the Howler where we left it, beside the closet. The closet door stood wide open.

"Could we grab the Howler and get out of here?" Justin asked. His voice cracked from fear.

I didn't have a chance to answer him.

A high shriek—deafening and shrill as a whistle—burst across the room.

I pressed my hands over my ears as the shriek grew louder, higher. A sharp pain shot through my head—behind my eyes—until it felt as if my eyes were going to pop out.

"Let's go!" I shouted. But my voice was drowned out by the deafening wail.

And then the ghosts appeared. Five howling figures, dancing out from the open closet. I saw a man and woman, another woman who was very old, and a boy and a girl. They wore old-fashioned clothes, tattered and faded.

Their pale gray skin was pulled tight against their skulls. Patches of skin had fallen away, revealing yellowed bone underneath. Clumps of spidery hair sprouted from their bald scalps.

Heads tossed back, they howled together, one ear-shattering note. They howled and danced, holding hands. A joyful dance. A dance of triumph.

Their heavy, old-fashioned shoes pounded the attic floor—but made no sound. At first, caught up in their frantic steps, they didn't seem to notice us.

But the old woman's eyes locked on me. She stopped her wild dance. The others stopped too. The attic air turned frigid and sour.

So silent now I could hear my heart hammering against my chest.

I spun away and started to run. Scott was already halfway down the stairs. Ed, Justin, and Vanessa were right behind me.

We stumbled down the attic stairs and ran. The shrill, ghostly wails started up again. Following us. Growing higher, louder, more excited—so close behind.

My breath escaped in wheezing gasps as I ran. The stairs, the walls, the rooms—all a bouncing blur in my throbbing head.

I followed Scott to the kitchen. He reached the back door first. Grabbed the doorknob—

—and let out a scream of pain.

"It's stuck! My hand is stuck!"

He tugged and squirmed. Then he tried pulling his hand off the knob with his other hand.

"Help me! OWWWWW! It's starting to burn!"

Ed and Justin didn't move. They gaped at Scott's hand—their eyes bulging.

Vanessa and I pushed past them. Scott's palm was stuck tightly to the brass knob. His fingers had turned bright red. As we stared, they darkened to purple.

"Do something!" Scott wailed. "It's like it's glued!"

I carefully tried to pry his fingers up.

But Scott screamed in pain.

I grabbed his whole hand and tried to turn it, to slide it off the knob.

"It—it's not working," Scott moaned. "It's not coming loose. Let go, Spencer."

I tried to raise my hand away. "Oh, no!" I cried. I tugged again. I twisted my hand and pulled hard.

"OW! What are you doing?" Scott screamed. "Get off me! Get *off*!"

"My hand . . ." I groaned. "It's stuck to yours."

We both twisted our hands. And tugged. I gritted my teeth and pulled with all my strength.

But my palm was stuck tight to the back of Scott's hand. And his hand was pressed to the doorknob.

Behind us, the howls grew louder. The cold, putrid wind floated into the kitchen. I knew the screaming ghosts wouldn't be far behind.

Vanessa stepped up behind me. "Let me help," she said.

"NO!" I shouted. "Stay away! Don't touch us!"

Vanessa's eyes went wide with horror as she stared at Scott and me, our hands locked together.

Suddenly, the kitchen grew silent.

I turned my head—and saw the five ghosts, staring at us.

Staring at us with blank, glassy eyes.

They were a family. A ghost family. Grandmother, father and mother, two kids.

"They're—they're coming for us," Vanessa whispered.

Yes. They were moving quickly now. Floating silently around the kitchen counter.

Their empty eyes locked on us coldly. Their faces knotted in anger.

As they came toward us, I twisted my hand and tugged hard, trying to free myself. But I couldn't pull away.

I wanted to scream. But panic choked my throat.

Justin and Ed backed up against the wall. Vanessa hunched over, tensed her muscles, both hands tightened into fists.

"*Trapped . . .*" the old woman rasped at us. "*You are trapped.*"

Gliding so softly over the floor, they moved to surround us. And as they floated toward us, they changed.

The clumps of hair dropped off. Their faces melted completely away, revealing open-jawed, toothless skulls.

They floated out of their clothes.

I gasped.

No skin on their bodies. No skin at all.

Their bones rattled as they moved, clattering and grinding as bone scraped against bone.

And as they neared, they tossed back their skulls. Another hideous, high wail escaped their toothless mouths.

"*EEEEEEEEEEEEEEEEEE!*"

Not a living sound. The shriek of the dead. Filled

with pain and anger. An ancient cry finally finding its voice.

"EEEEEEEEEEEEEEEE!"

Shrieking, skull tossed back, bones clattering, the father leaped onto Justin.

The ghost girl floated over Vanessa. Vanessa swung her fists. But she couldn't keep the ghost girl away.

Scott and I struggled, tossed and squirmed. Bent together. Our hands burning. Stuck. No escape.

No escape . . .

The mother and the son lowered their shoulder bones, raised their bony arms, and attacked.

I opened my mouth to scream as the boy lowered his head and clamped his toothless jaw down on my shoulder.

Squirming, twisting, desperate to free my hand, I shut my eyes and waited for the pain to rack my body.

Waited . . .

Waited . . .

No pain. I opened my eyes. The boy's jaw had slid right through me!

He raised a bony hand. Tightened it into a fist. And drove his fist into my stomach.

But I felt nothing. His hand shot through me and came out the other side.

I turned to Vanessa, who jumped right through the skeletal ghost girl.

Justin struggled with the father, ducking, dodging. Justin's head shot through the father's chest. "I—I can't feel him!" Justin cried.

"They can't touch us!" Vanessa shouted. "They can't hurt us!"

"EEEEEEEEEEEEE!" The ghosts shrieked out their unhappiness, their fury.

"We can hurt you," the boy rasped, pointing his bony finger at Vanessa. "We will have plenty of time for that."

"Trapped . . ." the old woman repeated. She opened her toothless, rotted mouth and cackled. An ugly, dry coughing sound. "Trapped."

"You'll never leave the house!" the ghost father cried.

"Our house! Our prison!" the mother shrieked. "Now it will be yours!"

Shrieking and cackling, the ghosts faded away.

The sudden silence was almost as frightening as their ugly cries. My eyes darted around the kitchen. The ghosts had vanished—but for how long?

"Hey!" I let out a startled cry as I realized my hand was free.

Scott stood up too, holding his hand, shaking it. His hand was purple and swollen. "It . . . came off the knob!"

I gazed down at my hand, tenderly squeezing it, moving the fingers until the ache started to fade. "Maybe when the ghosts left, they freed us."

"I don't care!" Scott cried. "Let's go!" He tried the door again. "It still won't open!"

"Now what?" Vanessa demanded.

"We can go out a window," Scott said. "The den window is easy."

"Yes!" I cried, pumping my fist in the air.

We started running toward the den. But I stopped in the living room.

My eye caught something on the table beside the couch. "The phone!" I shouted.

I flew across the room. "We can call for help. Someone can come and get us out of here!"

"Hurry—please!" Vanessa begged.

"Yes!" I lifted the phone—and punched in 911.

I pushed the emergency number, then pressed the phone to my ear and listened.

Silence for a second or two. And then . . .

"Hahahahahaha!" A high, shrill cackling laugh, tinny and distant-sounding.

I jerked the phone from my ear. But the ugly laughter continued to pour out of it.

With an angry grunt, I tossed the phone to the floor. "We can't call out," I told my friends. I could still hear the tinny laughter rising from the phone.

"Let's just get *out* of here!" Justin cried. "Why are we standing around?"

He took off running, into the den. We followed close behind.

Behind the couch, the den window looked out on the side of the house. Justin leaned over the couch and reached to pull up the window.

"No—don't touch it!" I shouted.

Justin pulled back.

"It might be hot or something," I warned.

Justin's eyes were wild. His face was bright red. "Then let's just break the glass and jump out," he said breathlessly.

He dove to the fireplace across the room and grabbed up a black wrought-iron fireplace poker. He raised it high in front of him and went charging toward the window.

Halfway across the room, he stopped short. His eyes bulged, and his mouth dropped open in a startled cry.

The fireplace poker dropped from his hand and clattered to the floor.

"Justin—what's wrong?" I cried.

He didn't answer. He shot out his arms and tensed his legs, trying to move. Grunting, he lowered his shoulder, as if trying to butt something out of his way.

He struggled and strained. But he couldn't move.

Was it some kind of invisible wall? A ghostly force holding him in place?

I lurched forward and reached out to help him.

Too late.

The force that held Justin spun him around—and slammed him headfirst into the wall.

THUDDDDDD.

I'll never forget the sound of Justin's head crashing so hard against the wood-paneled wall.

Holding my breath, I waited for him to bounce off. To fall to the floor.

But he didn't fall.

His head . . .

His head kept going . . . shooting into the wall.

His head vanished into the wood. And then his shoulders slid in after his head.

As if he had been fired from a cannon, I thought. As if the wall were swallowing him up, swallowing him whole.

His body disappeared up to his waist. His legs dangled in the air. He kicked his feet, struggling, struggling helplessly as he disappeared into the wall.

"Stop him! Save him!" Ed screamed. "Don't let him go!"

With a desperate cry, Ed leaped forward. He grabbed Justin around the ankles.

With a groan, he pulled back, tugged with all his strength.

"I . . . I can't . . . stop . . . it," Ed whispered.

Justin's sneakers snapped into the wall.

I uttered a cry as Ed's hands were sucked in too.

Ed screamed and screamed again.

His arms slid into the wood as if being pulled by a powerful force.

And then Ed's screams were cut off as his head smacked the wall. A wet *squish*—and then Ed's head shot into the wall.

His shoulders disappeared.

His whole body.

His shoes thudded hard against the wood. Then vanished.

Vanished.

My two friends. Gone.

Scott, Vanessa, and I stared at the wood-paneled wall.

Smooth now. Not a mark. Not a scratch. Not a hole where the two bodies were sucked in.

"Wh-where did they go?" Vanessa choked out.

Scott dropped to his knees on the carpet, his body racked with shudder after shudder. "Are . . . are they dead? Are they *ghosts* now? Is this what the ghost family plans to do to all of us?"

My heart hammered against my chest. I couldn't take my eyes off the den wall. Are they gone forever? I wondered. No trace of them? Nothing left at all?

I turned to the fireplace poker on the floor. I wanted to grab it up and start swinging it.

I wanted to batter down the wall and find my friends. Then I wanted to keep swinging it. And swinging it and swinging it.

I wanted to batter down the ghosts that were doing this to us.

But my fear soon overcame my anger.

There were only three of us left. Only three.

We had to be very careful.

"What should we do now?" Vanessa whispered. "Any ideas?"

Before Scott or I could answer, we heard a sound. A car horn honk. From the front.

We ran to the living room window—in time to see a car pulling up the driveway.

"My parents!" Scott cried.

We watched their blue Saturn crunch up the snow-covered driveway, heading to the garage at the back of the house. Scott's dad honked the horn again, letting Scott know he was home.

"We've got to warn them," Scott said, his eyes wide with fear. "We've got to warn them to stay away."

He started running to the back, but I grabbed him by the shoulders and held him back. "No, Scott—wait," I pleaded. "This could be our chance. Maybe our last chance."

He spun around. "You mean—"

"Maybe they can open the door from the outside," Vanessa said excitedly. "We can't let ourselves out. But maybe *they* can let us out."

I heard a car door slam. Then another. Scott's parents were climbing out of the car, making their way to the kitchen door.

We ran to the kitchen. Outside the window, I could see them. They had stopped beside the driveway to examine a section of hedge that was tilting.

"Hurry!" I called. "Please—hurry!"

Then I heard a startled shout. I turned from the window to see Scott start to spin.

"Help me!" he screamed. His arms flew straight out. His black hair whipped around as his whole body began to spin. Faster, faster. Like a top picking up speed.

"Help me!" His cry faint now, muffled by the powerful wind around him as he whirled. Whirled helplessly, caught in an invisible force that hurled him around and around.

"Ohhhh . . . hellllp."

I saw his twirling feet leave the floor.

Vanessa grabbed my arm as we stared in horror. Stared at Scott—spinning faster, faster—so fast, he had become a blur of color.

Up, up—to the kitchen ceiling.

"Oh, no," I whispered, seeing the ceiling bubble. The kitchen ceiling was liquid now. A creamy, white, bubbling liquid.

The ceiling made a sick sucking sound as Scott's spinning head poked into it. The creamy liquid bubbled and puckered.

Spinning harder, Scott's body shot up into the wet ceiling.

His arms dangled crazily, fluttering around him. His legs kicked at the swirling air.

Sploooosh.

Another heavy sucking sound as his shoulders slid up into the bubbling, wet ceiling.

In seconds, he was gone.

The ceiling grew hard and smooth again.

No sign of him. No sign at all.

Vanessa and I stared at each other. Her hand still gripped my arm. We were both trembling.

"We're the only two left," Vanessa whispered.

And then we staggered to the kitchen door. Careful to stay a foot or two back. And we started to scream to Scott's parents.

"Help us!"

"Please—hurry!"

"Get us out!"

Scott's parents turned away from the hedge. Their faces filled with confusion. They glanced all around, as if trying to figure out where the voices were coming from.

Finally, Scott's mom saw Vanessa and me through the window in the kitchen door. Her mouth dropped open in surprise. She grabbed her husband's hand and pointed to Vanessa and me.

"Hurry—please!" Vanessa shouted. "Open the door!"

They started to jog across the snow. I could see their breath puffing up in white clouds as they ran.

They took four or five steps before they started to sink.

Both of them cried out at the same time.

Their hands flew up. Scott's mom's pocketbook went sailing into the snow.

They sank so fast.

The snow splashed up all around them, as if they had stepped into a big puddle. I could hear the *whoooosh* from inside the house.

They were surrounded by tall waves of sparkling white snow. And then, as the waves fell back to the ground, Scott's parents dropped with them.

They both uttered shrill screams of horror and shock.

They screamed as they slid down . . . down.

They thrashed their arms wildly, grasping at the ground. Struggling to keep their heads above the surface. Slapping the snow. Slapping it frantically.

Screaming . . . screaming.

I could hear the screams even after their heads had vanished beneath the snow.

Then silence.

The snow lay flat and smooth. A soft wind sent a spray of glittering powder over the ground.

Silence.

Shivering, our bodies trembling, Vanessa and I turned to each other. All alone now.

All alone in a house filled with angry ghosts. Ghosts eager to have their revenge.

I turned away from the kitchen door. I didn't want to see the smooth snow. The snow that had just swallowed Scott's parents.

Our last hope.

"What do we do now?" Vanessa asked in a tiny voice. "Just wait for them to get us too?"

Her question sent a chill down my back.

I could hear the creak of floorboards in the front of the house. I heard whispers. Snickering laughter. And the soft scrape of ghostly footsteps.

Were they coming for us now?

Would we disappear the way the others had?

I tried to imagine what it would feel like to be jammed headfirst into the wall. Or sucked into the ceiling.

How much would that hurt?

I shut my eyes. Panic made my mind whirl with crazy thoughts. Where could we hide? How do you hide from ghosts?

Even if we did hide, how long could we stay alive in this haunted house?

"The Howler." The words burst suddenly from my throat.

I opened my eyes and gazed at Vanessa. "Yes. The Howler," I repeated.

"What about it?" Vanessa whispered.

"Maybe we can reverse it. Send those ghosts back into the closet."

Vanessa shook her head unhappily. "It won't work, Spencer. The Howler didn't summon the ghosts. The Howler didn't help them escape. We pulled open the closet door—remember? That's how

123

they escaped. The Howler only let us hear their howls."

I stared at her, my mind spinning. She was right.

But I had another idea. "Ian. What if I can use the Howler to reach Ian?" I said. "Would he help us get out of here?"

I grabbed Vanessa's hand and started to pull her to the stairs. "Hurry. The ghosts won't give us much time. Maybe . . . maybe we can reach him."

"It's worth a try," Vanessa said. And then she added in a trembling voice, "I guess."

We made our way up to the attic. Outside, the sun had lowered behind the trees. The attic stood in darkness.

I expected to see them—the ghost family—floating toward us, shimmering in the gray-blue dark. Howling. Their skeletal faces glowing with their anger.

But the attic was empty and silent.

Keeping close together, Vanessa and I crossed the room to the Howler on the carton where we had left it. We knelt down in front of it.

I turned the power button and watched the yellow dial flash on. I gave it a few seconds to warm up.

Would it work? It was a crazy idea. But our friends had all disappeared. Vanessa and I were next. I was desperate.

I brought my face close to the speaker. I pushed the red button.

"Hello?" My voice came out tiny and weak.

"Hello?" I tried again. "Ian? It's me—Spencer. Are you there? Can you hear me?"

Silence.

I felt Vanessa's icy hand on my shoulder. "This is so crazy," she murmured.

I leaned back toward the Howler and called into it. "Hello? Ian? Please! Ian—are you there?"

Vanessa and I stared into the glowing yellow dial, waiting for a reply. Waiting . . .

This isn't going to work, I realized. I'm just wasting time.

We're doomed. Doomed.

That was my last thought—my last, gloomy thought—before the Howler exploded.

The Howler exploded without warning.

I didn't hear the blast until after I had been shot backward—lifted off my feet—and thrown against the attic wall.

I let out a weak groan as the crash took my breath away.

The flash of flame was so bright, I could see it through my closed eyelids.

And then, as the pain raced over my body, swallowing me, devouring me—I heard the explosion. A blast of sound that rattled my bones, that made my teeth vibrate.

The attic rocked from side to side. I saw another tall burst of flames. And then everything went black.

I opened my eyes to a shimmering wall of yellow and orange flames.

I sucked in a deep breath and started to cough. Thick black smoke choked the attic.

"I'm . . . alive," I murmured. My back and shoulders ached. But I felt my strength returning.

I had fallen into a sitting position against the wall. I pulled myself to my feet.

Flames crackled and danced, leaping to the attic ceiling.

"Vanessa?" I called, my voice hoarse from the smoke. "Vanessa—are you okay?"

She came staggering toward me through the swirling smoke. Black cinders clung to her hair. Her sweater was ripped, and I saw a deep cut on her right shoulder.

"Out. Have to get out," she whispered, holding her throat.

Flames. Dancing flames all around. Behind them, the walls appeared to be melting, like wax on a burning candle.

I felt dizzy. I turned, searching for the stairway.

And as I turned, I saw the faces. The faces of the ghost family in the melting wall.

The brother and sister, their parents, the grandmother. I could see them so clearly through the flames. Laughing. Laughing and howling. The ugly sounds rose up over the crackle of the flames.

And then the howling ghosts floated off the wall. And came rushing toward Vanessa and me.

We didn't say a word. We turned and, choking on the thick, bitter smoke, started to run.

Vanessa reached the stairs first. We both hurled ourselves down.

The howls and laughter followed us as we ran.

We reached the second-floor landing and dove for the stairs.

Cackling, howling like wolves, the ghost family chased after us.

Vanessa and I staggered into the living room—and were greeted by another explosion. The walls shook. The curtains flew up. The front window shattered. Glass flew in all directions.

Behind us, I saw the ghost family float down the stairs. They were covered in flames. The red and orange flames leaped off their bodies.

The five ghosts stared at us as they moved across the room. Stared at us with empty eyes. Dark holes where their eyes should be. As they came closer, I could see flames flickering in their empty eye sockets.

I turned back to Vanessa and pointed. "The window. We can get out now."

We dove out through the shattered front window, toppling into the snow.

The cold shocked my body. I jumped up, shivering.

Vanessa was already on her feet. She grabbed my hand and tugged me toward the street.

We ran over the hardened snow, our shoes slipping and sliding. My wheezing breaths steamed up in front of me.

Were the ghosts chasing after us?

Yes.

I glanced back and saw them burst out of the window—an explosion of howling flames. They rolled over the snow, clamoring after us on all fours like wild animals. And as they ran, the flames died, and their bodies turned blue.

I gaped at the five glowing blue figures, howling, cackling, wailing, as they galloped over the snow.

I spun away and ran to catch up to Vanessa. She was halfway up the block and picking up speed, her red hair flapping wildly behind her.

We reached the lake and kept running. It was as if an invisible force had pulled us here. We didn't stop to think. We raced over the icy surface.

And then it was too late.

The ghosts didn't hesitate at the shore. They rolled onto the ice, pulling themselves up onto two legs. Gliding so easily, their empty eyes on us.

"Wh-where can we go?" Vanessa cried, pressing her hands to her face. "We made a terrible mistake."

We ran farther out, our shoes kicking up snow from the hard, gray ice.

"Maybe we can outrun them," I gasped, struggling to catch my breath. "If we can get past them . . . get back to shore . . ." My voice trailed off.

It's hopeless, I thought. *We were so stupid.*

Glowing a cold, frozen blue, the ghosts circled us. Their laughter rang out over the ice and echoed off the trees at the shore.

They knew they had us trapped.

They floated in on us, howling, shaking their fists.

And as they moved in, they circled us faster. Faster . . .

They whirled around us, a cold blue cyclone.

I heard the *craack* of the ice.

The ghosts circled faster and began to twirl.

"They're—they're heating the ice!" I cried.

Another ripping *craaaack*.

The ice buckled and cracked. I could see it split beneath us.

"We're—we're going under!" I screamed.

I tried to move. But I could feel the ice give way beneath me.

The ghosts kept circling, twirling faster and faster.

The ice cracked again. A deep crack this time. I could feel it splitting, shifting, about to fall away.

I sucked in a deep breath and prepared to sink.

Craaaaack.

A slab of ice tilted straight up. I saw tossing, dark water underneath it.

And then I saw . . .

I saw . . .

A boy come floating over the broken ice. A boy bathed in a blue glow.

His arms were crossed in front of his down vest. His body rose stiffly, his back straight, every muscle tensed.

I recognized him at once.

"Ian!" I cried. "Ian! It was you! It was you I saw skating that night on the ice!"

I suddenly felt so happy, so glad to see him—until I caught the cold, angry expression on his face. Through the blue glow, I could see his eyes narrowed in fury, his mouth twisted in an angry scowl.

He raised his arms stiffly and staggered toward me, ready to strangle me.

"No, Ian! Please!" I screamed. "Ian! Don't!"

The ghost family stopped twirling. They huddled in a line now, their vacant eyes on Ian.

Ian's hands were balled into tight fists. He took another step over the ice, and I realized he was wearing ice skates.

My brother's ice skates. The ones Ian drowned in.

"Ian—please!" I begged, staring at his wet blue face. "I tried to save you. I really did!"

He took another stiff, menacing step.

Finally, he spoke. "I know you tried, Spencer." His voice was muffled, a faint whisper, as if from far away. "You risked your life for me. You nearly drowned too."

He took another step forward. "That's why I stayed around," he said. "I've been here all along. I wanted to thank you for trying to save me. But I was so weak . . . too weak to contact you."

"You—you've been here all year?" I whispered.

He nodded. "But I was too weak. Too weak . . .

Finally, I felt strong enough to reach you. I tried to let you know I was here."

"I—I don't understand," I said.

"That night on the frozen lake. I found a glove on the ice. I put it on and tried to grab you. But I was so weak. . . ."

"That was you!" I gasped.

"And the red paint," Ian continued. "I tried to paint my name on your wall. But I grew too tired after I painted the I. And then at dinner, I tried to call to you. But I could only whisper. I couldn't make you hear me."

"It was YOU!" I cried again. "It was you all along! I thought—"

"Last night, I tried to put on your suit," Ian said. "I thought maybe then you could see me better. But I only frightened you."

"Ian, I'm so sorry—" I started.

But his eyes were on the five ghosts. "I'm here to help you now," he said softly. And then he stepped past me and began to skate.

The five ghosts tried to back away. They tilted back their heads and roared. I covered my ears. The roar sounded like a hundred angry lions. The sound made the trees shake and bend.

Ian bent forward and skated so fast, he was a blue blur. His blades scraped and sliced, cutting deeply into the ice.

He circled the roaring ghosts. Circled them again.

As Vanessa and I stared in amazement, Ian cut a deep circle in the ice. The ice cracked and split. And the circle slid down . . . down . . . until it bobbed under the water.

Roaring, howling, clawing the air, the ghost family plunged into the water.

It happened so fast. A tall splash of dark water. Just one splash.

And the ghosts were gone. The roars, the howls—cut off.

I could see the blue glow under the water. And then steam began to rise up from the hole Ian had cut.

White steam shot up like a geyser. Thicker. Thicker. The steam spread out. Washed over the lake. Swept over Vanessa and me.

Thick, choking steam. So hot . . . sizzling over the ice . . .

When it finally cleared, I blinked several times and rubbed my eyes. I looked down to see that the ice was solid again.

The ghosts were gone.

"Ian?" I called. "Ian—are you still here?"

No.

Ian had also vanished.

The evergreens stood tall and silent on the shore. Two large birds circled overhead. The wind blew waves of powdery snow over the ice.

Normal. Everything seemed normal again.

Vanessa and I began to run to shore. A few minutes later, we reached the street and kept running.

"Normal." I kept repeating the word in my mind. Repeating it until it became a prayer. Please—let everything be normal again.

And it was.

Scott's house stood, as always, next door to mine. No exploded window. No sign of a fire.

As Vanessa and I raced up the driveway, Scott, Ed, and Justin came running out. "Where did you two go?" Scott demanded. "What's up with you guys?"

Scott didn't remember anything that had happened. None of them did.

I tore up to the attic. Dark and silent. No fire. No ghosts. The Howler stood on the carton where I'd left it. I picked it up and examined it. No sign that it had exploded.

Everyone seemed eager to get home. We all said goodbye. Vanessa and I exchanged glances. We were the only ones who remembered the horror, who knew that we had all just barely survived.

I carried the Howler home and up to my room. I promised myself that my adventures with ghosts were over.

I had seen Ian. Ian had forgiven me. And he had saved my life. I hoped he could rest now.

I wrapped the cord tightly around the Howler. The little box was dangerous. Deadly dangerous. I planned to hide it away in the basement, where no one could find it.

But before I could step out of my room, Nick barged in. "Hey, punk—" he greeted me. "Is that your face, or were you hit by a truck?"

"Ha-ha," I muttered. "Funny. Real funny."

"Give me that thing," Nick said, grabbing for the Howler.

"No way," I replied, jerking it away.

"No. Give it to me," Nick insisted. "Remember that joke I played on you with it? When I made you scream like a stupid baby? I want to play that same trick on some girls I know."

I hesitated. I opened my mouth to explain to my brother just how dangerous the Howler could be.

"Hand it over, punk," he growled. "Or I'll pound you till your face looks like coleslaw."

After that, I couldn't help it. I couldn't keep a grin from spreading over my face.

"Okay, here," I said, giving the Howler to Nick. "Take it. Have fun. Have a lot of fun."

ABOUT THE AUTHOR

R.L. STINE says he has a great job. "My job is to give kids the CREEPS!" With his scary books, R.L. has terrified kids all over the world. He has sold over 300 million books, making him the best-selling children's author in history.

These days, R.L. is dishing out new frights in his series THE NIGHTMARE ROOM. When he isn't working, he likes to read old mysteries, watch *SpongeBob Squarepants* on TV, and take his dog, Nadine, for long walks around New York City, where he lives with his wife, Jane, and son, Matthew.

"I love taking my readers to scary places," R.L. says. "Do you know the scariest place of all? It's your MIND!"

Take a look at what's ahead in
THE NIGHTMARE ROOM #8
Shadow Girl

I pulled open the door. The room behind it was totally dark.

I took a step inside and swept my hand over the wall, searching for a light switch.

Stan stepped in behind me. He huddled so close, he bumped into me.

"Okay!" I found the switch and clicked it on. A ceiling light flashed on, sending bright yellow light over us.

Blinking against the sudden light, I glanced around.

The room was not much bigger than a closet. It was completely bare, no furniture at all. The ratty, brown carpet had a long tear in it. The gray paint on the walls was peeling.

A window on the wall across from us was covered by a wide, black shade. A single, wooden shelf was built into the wall next to the window. It appeared to have something resting on it.

Stan pulled off his ski cap and shoved it into his coat pocket. His brown hair was matted wetly to his forehead.

"Why would Jada come in *here*?" he asked. "It's just an empty closet."

I shrugged. "Beats me. I'm totally confused. I thought we'd find something really interesting."

I stepped past Stan and crossed to the shelf on the wall. I saw a dark pile of cloth folded neatly on the shelf.

No. Not cloth.

I pulled part of it down and unfolded it. A long, blue-black cloak.

I held it out in front of me. "Check this out, Stan. It's like a cape with a hood."

"Weird," he said, studying it. He pulled the rest of the stuff off the shelf. "Look." He held up a pair of black tights. Long, silky black gloves. An oval-shaped, blue pendant on a chain. And then a mask. A black mask with two cat-eye holes cut into the front.

"Must be some kind of Halloween costume," he said.

I took the mask from him and rolled it around in my hands. "Why would anyone leave a Halloween costume back here in a hidden room?" I asked.

I slid the mask under the hood of the cloak. And then another idea struck me. "It looks like some kind of superhero costume," I said. "*The Masked Cape Person*!"

Stan still had the black tights in his hand. "Yeah. Well, I guess that's what superheroes wear, right? Tights and a cape?"

I raised the cloak in front of me. "Do you think this is Jada's? Think she wears this stuff?"

Stan shook his head. His face was knotted in confusion.

I laughed. "Maybe Jada has a secret life that no one knows about. Maybe she sneaks in here at night, and puts on this costume, and *pretends* to be The Masked Cape Person!"

Stan shook his head. "This is just too weird," he said again.

And then his expression changed. His eyes went wide. He suddenly turned pale. "Selena—" he whispered, staring at the mask in my hand.

"What? What's wrong?" I asked.

"What if—what if that's a *burglar* costume?"

I let out a gasp. "Excuse me?"

"It looks like something a burglar might wear," Stan said. "And didn't they say on the news—"

"That the person who has been robbing houses in Elmwood wore a mask and a cape?" I cut in.

Stan nodded excitedly.

"But that's totally insane!" I cried. "Jada a burglar? That's too stupid, Stan. She's a twelve-year-old girl, like me. She doesn't put on a costume and sneak out in the middle of the night to rob houses."

I moved to the window and tugged on the shade until it slid up. Gray light washed into the room. The window had been left open a crack.

I peered outside. A high tree branch rested right

outside. It would be easy for someone to climb out this window, onto the tree branch—and then climb down to the ground.

What was I thinking?

"You are *so* not right," I told Stan. "No way my cousin is a burglar!"

Stan nodded. "Yeah. It's a stupid idea. Don't ever tell Jada I said it."

He started to fold up the tights. "I don't think we solved the mystery, Selena."

"We made the mystery even more mysterious," I said. I tugged down the shade. Then I started to fold the cloak.

"Hey—is anybody home?" a voice called.

Stan and I both gasped.

Jada's voice. From downstairs.

We were caught.